LIKE CLOCKWORK

A Steampunk Adventure of Love and Terror

Wayne Tripp

LIKE CLOCKWORK

By Wayne Tripp

© 2015 Wayne Tripp

5174 Peri Street
Swartz Creek, MI 48473

Cover design by Clarissa Yeo

Printed in United States of America

I'd like to dedicate Like Clockwork to my soul mate, Robin, the true heroine in my life. Also to Jules Verne, Robert Louis Stevenson and Sir Arthur Conan Doyle, who ignited the spark that made me dream.

CHAPTER ONE

"Are you t-there?"

"We're here, Miss. Are you all right?"

"Y-yes. He's gone to fetch more beer." Kathleen saw no need to volunteer that she'd already had to defend her honor twice during the hansom cab ride to North Street. Her disheveled corset and rumpled shirtwaist bore silent witness to her desperate resistance.

"I'll be all right." Glancing at the small, walnut box of dials, copper wires and whirring brass gears nestled in her gloved hand, she softly added, "I-I gather the aether-speak is working, Sgt. Murphy."

"Yes, it is. It's working just fine, Miss. We can hear everything quite clearly on the aether-speak," the gruff sergeant said, blushing to the roots of his cauliflower ears and quite enjoying the soft lilt of her Irish brogue so reminiscent of the old country. "Just keep the aetherways open. You do have the wee derringer, don't you, Miss?"

"Yes, thank you, Patrick."

"Remember, should the bugger try anything, me and the boys are just itching to jump to your rescue. Just holler, Miss."

"I know, Patrick. And thanks. Oops—he's coming back. I've got to go."

* * * *

A half hour later, outside the *Clockwork Barmaid*, they were in a shadow-filled alley just north of infamous Dock Square, looking to any casual observer like two drunken lovers waiting for a passing cab. Kathleen had hoped they were bound for some late night entertainment in a crowded music hall. Lots of people. Lots of witnesses. Suddenly, her companion slapped his palms against the wall on either side of her narrow shoulders, imprisoning her. He was really starting to frighten her. As he slammed Katie back against the grimy brick like a common dollymop, she realized with a twinge of paralyzing panic, he felt *she* should provide the entertainment.

Testimony she'd been caught off-guard yet again, she barely managed to bat his groping, swarthy hands away before dropping her aether-speak, and letting loose with a blood-curdling scream for help. A good Catholic girl, Katie believed in the doctrine that the Lord helps those who help themselves. Raising one black high-buttoned shoe she tried to connect with the huge unmentionable between his legs. He turned sideways, his thick thigh absorbing the blow. Her ineffective efforts only excited him. He increased his efforts. When she felt his cold, damp hand shove up her skirts and tear at her undergarments, she shook her head and screamed again, clawing at him with her nails.

It took far too many precious minutes for the first team of coppers to respond to her screams.

* * * *

"Wildethorne, come in. Constable Wildethorne, are you bloody there? Answer me, you damned bugger!"

Sergeant Murphy slapped the small aether-speak receiver into his ham-sized palm repeatedly as if shaking dirt out of the earpiece. "Damn it, come in. You're the closest team, and McBride is in trouble. You've got to hear her screaming, you damned Yankee dunderhead."

Minutes later, a bleary voice much the worse for recent drinking mumbled into the small communicator.

"Hallo, Sergeant Murffy. We're here on Fish Street. At our post as instructed. Wat can I do fur you, Sgt. Murffy? Oops." There was the sound of fumbling and curses as the person at the other end of the aetherlink dropped his communication device. Quite obviously, Officer Wildethorne was well beyond assisting anyone, including himself.

"Drunk again, heh, Wildethorne? Jeezus! And I suppose that useless bugger with you, O'Rourke, has found hisself a nice hole to snooze in. Be at the precinct by seven. I'll see to you both first thing in the morning." Sgt. Murphy broke the connection without waiting for a reply and immediately contacted the team waiting on distant Ship Street, already knowing in his heart that they'd failed in their protective duties and Miss McBride would most likely become the "Rude Ruffian's" latest victim.

* * * *

Dragged two city blocks away, below the level of the crumpled brick sidewalk in a deserted, dimly-lit cellar festooned with spider webs and stinking of cat urine, semi-conscious Katie McBride stirred in her torn petticoats just long enough to utter a single curse. "Damn you, Scott."

Looking around her, Katie could just make out several of the crude obscene drawings the Rude Ruffian was known for. *Darn stupid moniker the press gave you in light of the disgusting, things you do, you monster. Looks like I drew out the right bastard at least. Great. Sister Catherine of St. Margaret's Academy would be so proud of her star pupil God, where were the damned coppers?*

It wasn't a peeler who suddenly grabbed her shoulder and tried to push her back down to the damp concrete floor. Kathleen McBride channeled her rage and refused to give up. Determined not to die like her friend Bridget at the hands of the fiend the Boston press had dubbed the "Rude Ruffian", she punched at him like a frantic hellcat. Catching a fist full of his curly black hair, she managed to scratch his olive-skinned cheek. She fought like an enraged mongoose cornered by a cobra. He backed away, dropping the whirring and blinking turbo blade he'd pulled from his pocket and cursing her from a safe distance. The hand he put to his cheek came away bloody. He held it up to examine it and cursed again. The glare he shot at Katie sent chills slithering down her spine.

It was at this point the coppers from the precinct showed up. In the confined excitement, they filled the shadowy cellar with poorly aimed shots of whizzing lead. Katie screamed. Her attacker spun around, cursing in his foreign tongue and desperately looking for an escape. Finding none, he cursed again, his hands shooting up in surrender. The nearest officer grabbed him and snapped on matching steel bracelets, which brought to a close Katie's brief, unhappy police adventure.

* * * *

The next day, the scuttlebutt around the precinct virtually ignored the killer's capture, centering on the loud expulsion of constables Wildethorne and O'Rourke, *and* the delightful display of Miss McBride's near-naked bosom at the crime scene. This no doubt prompted the precinct chief to feel obligated to alert her parents to their daughter's clandestine under-cover activity

* * * *

A week passed, chased away by several more. No word came from Scott. It was as though he'd dropped off the planet. Katie was miserable. Her parents seemed to find it hard to forgive her. Sean, her Papa, barely grunted at her as he perused his morning paper and slurped his coffee at the breakfast table. Mum had finally hugged her, doing her ritualistic thing smoothing and pinning Katie's wayward red tresses into a more presentable bun. But then had come the daily pilgrimage to St. Paul's cathedral. Maeve McBride made darned sure her wayward daughter accompanied her to early morning Mass.

A second month began, and still no word from Scott. The days were growing easier to endure; her parents seemed to feel they could all sit together in the main parlor for a few hours without harping on the misfortune she'd all forced them to endure. Katie moped around their comfortable home, bored with the fancy needlework and piano lessons her mother assured her were the golden arrows found in the quiver of every successful, proper young lady. She longed for the gritty shadow world she'd glimpsed during her brush with undercover police work. She longed for Scott Wildethorne. *Oh just to hear the sound of his voice. His rich, throaty laughter. The look in his eyes when he looked at her.* She vowed to find an excuse to call him on the family aether-speak, or better yet, take a horseless cab and go visit him. *If only Mother didn't watch her like a hawk!*

One morning she woke up sick to her stomach. She barely had time to gather up the folds of her nightdress and reach for her chamber pot before vomiting. Not wanting to disturb her mother, she managed to dispose of the bowl's contents without troubling the gossipy upstairs maid.

The following morning brought the same stomach misery, only this time she felt so woozy, so terribly ill, she hadn't a chance to empty the pot. The maid did, and wasted no time informing Mistress McBride. Mother descended on Katie like a worried clucking hen, and within hours she was packed off to visit Dr.

O'Brien. Her mum was beside herself, fearful it was a bout of the virulent influenza she'd heard was plaguing South Boston.

The visit to Dr. O'Brien's plush office began by calming her mother's fears; it wasn't influenza. The family had been tiptoeing around on eggshells for months, trying to salvage some of their lofty social standing among the elite of Boston, and rebuild an air of normalcy. Katie had been among the most desirable blooming young ladies of Boston, blessed with a lovely face and figure and coming from a highly esteemed, respectable and prosperous family. An indiscreet behavior on her part coupled with an unforgiveable leak on the part of the police had badly tarnished the family's reputation.

Katie was damaged goods. Who would want her now? In spite of their stubborn daughter, Katie's parents had been striving desperately to revitalize her marriage prospects. Invited to three evening soirees and a night at the ballet during the last week, things were finally starting to perk up.

Yet, the doctor's final diagnosis, determined by the very latest in scientific gadgetry, shattered all those fragile eggs with a single sentence. Their rebellious daughter, Kathleen Erin McBride had apparently lied about the ending to her sordid police adventure. She had been despoiled by the depraved Rude Ruffian after all.

Katie was quite pregnant.

Her morning sickness tapered off by the end of the month, but by then the damage was done. Katie's mum never missed an opportunity to remind her no one would want her now. At least, no one who mattered.

There was still no word from Scott. Katie managed to contact his police partner on the aether-speak, and found out the irate chief had chewed them both out and kicked them off the force. Scott had wasted no time hanging around. He was gone. Tim O'Rourke hadn't seen hide nor hair of him since, not even in their favorite drinking dives down by the waterfront.

Katie knew where Scott lived in Boston and thought maybe he'd shut himself up there. No one would tell her anything more than he'd been fired for drinking. *Mother Mary, she hoped he wasn't drinking himself to death. Him and his rotgut rum.* He'd told her he had people in southeastern Massachusetts, or was it Rhode Island? Silently, Katie prayed she'd find him in the Boston apartment. If he wasn't there, he was truly gone.

With tears choking her voice, she tried to end the conversation with Tim O'Rourke. The maid had already wandered by her secluded window seat twice, obviously curious. Tim droned on, making it quite plain he was already cozying up to his ale. He said he was sorry he couldn't help, but it was as if the earth had opened up and swallowed Scott whole. Always the policeman, he did some pumping of his own. Why did Katie want to find Scott anyway?

Katie mumbled her good-byes and thumped down the aether-speak before O'Rourke could cause her to break down, revealing how much she missed Scott, the scoundrel.

* * * *

All she needed was a day free of her mother's relentless surveillance. It finally came gift-wrapped three days later, a one-time opportunity to take advantage of her mum's day-long migraine that sequestered her to a darkened bedroom. Three trolley and one hansom cab ride later, she had slipped her shackles and arrived at Scott's waterfront apartment. It was not a nice neighborhood. Idle doxies and dollymops watched her from shadowy windowsills and doorways. Giggling at the scandalized look on her mum's face if she had an inkling of where she was and what she was about to do, Katie double-checked the address she'd jotted down on the scrap of paper with the stained street sign. Two squawking sea gulls sitting atop the sign left little doubt as to what it was stained *with*.

Mermaid Lane. Twenty-nine Mermaid Lane. *This was the place, all right. What was she about to do? What would she say to him? What would he do? What had she been thinking!*

Realizing her courage was melting away as fast as a snowflake in a fireplace, Katie forced herself to open the tenement's battered door and work her way up to flights of rickety stairs. *As if being with child wasn't enough, she'd foolishly worn her corset laced tight—she could barely breathe!* Struggling to catch her breath, she read the dingy numbers stenciled on each dirty door until she spied 4B. She knocked several times, each time growing a little bolder, a little more desperate. *Where was he? He wasn't home. Oh God, why didn't he answer?*

The door behind her opened with such suddenness, Katie felt her heart skip a beat.

"What does yer want, luv? Oh—you be wanting Mr. Wildethorne? Can't say I blames ya, him being so nice and such a fine figure of a man. Tried ta get him in through my door once or twice, if you knows what I mean. Always said he was sweet on somebody already; someone with flame red hair. I reckon that be you, Dearie."

"I-is he here? In town?"

"Don't know about him being somewheres else. He ain't *here*. Been gone these many weeks now, mores the pity." The squat toad, face painted with far too much garish makeup, stopped and hawked a glob of thick phlegm right at Katie's booted feet. Running a heavily veined hand through her sparse white hair, the woman stared hard at Katie with watery grey eyes before continuing. She reeked of cheap booze.

"He left right after he got booted off the force. Upset him something fierce. I heared there was a woman involved. Him looking as fine as that, there'd have to be a woman involved, wouldn't there, dearie?" The old slattern scrutinized Katie again as though she was studying a bug under a magnifying glass. "I heared she was a good-looking young lady, much like yourself, Miss. You be her, dearie?"

Growing flustered, Katie stuttered a feeble good-bye and began stomping down the endless stairs, mindful of the biting ridge to her constricting corset. The old woman's harpy voice followed her down. "He's gone, dearie. Mr. Wildethorne is long gone."

Kathleen drifted home in a daze. Trolleys, cabs, she boarded them all without conscious thought. It was amazing she hadn't ended up in some alley, beaten, robbed . . . or worse. The automaton conductor of one downtown trolley had to ask her four times for her fare. As she finally handed him the coins, she could've sworn she smelt something electrical burning .*It didn't matter. She just didn't care. Scott was gone.* Her hopes collapsed and any plans she may have conjured lay in ruins. He was gone. The one man she'd secretly loved for so long was gone. Unconsciously touching the cheap locket she'd hidden beneath her chemise, she felt the first tears begin to fall. She'd hoped to share so much with Scott; he'd obviously never given her a second thought as he skipped out of her life forever. *Damn him!*

Blinded by her tears, Katie blundered into the Sunday parlor and under the leveled glares of both parents. Obviously, her mother had recovered from her headache.

"Where have you been, young lady?" Sean McBride roared. "Your poor mother and I have been worried sick!"

"I-I've been—Oh, mum," she blurted out before throwing herself into her mother's chill embrace. "I've been such a fool!"

"*Where* have you been . . . you young trollop? You were seen! Mrs. Baldwin saw you boarding a trolley near the waterfront. She says you appeared dazed, and your hair and clothes were disheveled. Who were you meeting there?" Sean bellowed. "Tell me!"

"Papa—please don't do this. You're upsetting me. Think of my baby."

"Your baby! Apparently you weren't thinking of your unfortunate . . . indiscretion. Or were you? Was it the child's father you went to visit? Tell me!"

"Sean! Dearest—calm yourself. Remember your heart. Keep in mind what Dr. O'Brien said about undue stress. We both *know* who the child's father is. That depraved monster in Walpole prison. He is, isn't her, Katie?"

"Y-yes, mummy. You know he is." Katie prayed her parents hadn't noticed her biting her lower lip, or the slight hesitancy in her voice. "I only wish I didn't know whose child it was."

"Well, my young gallivanting tart, you've embarrassed this family for the last time." Sean declared, slamming his fist down on an ornate Chippendale table to emphasize his point. Out of the corner of her eye, Katie saw her mother cringe and turn away. "Beside Elaine Baldwin, Father Murphy was coming to the house to see why you both missed mass this morning and saw you sneaking out on your little escapade. You know by tomorrow your silly adventure will be the talk of the entire parish. I will not let you ruin everything I've worked for since we came to this country," Sean shouted, punctuating each word with a fresh blow to the innocent table.

"What your father and I have decided," interjected Maeve McBride, with unusual steely resolve, "is to send you for a time to stay with my family in Newport. We need to repair the horrid damage you've done, young lady, before we can hope to retake our rightful place in Boston society."

"But mummy—I hate Newport! And I hate my uncle. He's so-so creepy! And . . . and I don't know anybody there. I'll be all alone. You can't do this!"

"We can and we shall," thumped her father.

"You won't be alone, dear. Aunt Agnes will be there. You liked her the last time we visited."

"That was three years ago. Besides, Aunt Agnes is stone deaf in both ears and has gout. Please, mummy–don't do this!"

They did.

Within the week, it was like Kathleen McBride had never been a resident of Boston.

The plan was for Katie to return after her unfortunate circumstances had been dealt with and forgotten. The time of her confinement, with just a few months beyond that for good measure. Just enough time to still the wagging tongues and let people find something new to gossip about.

Unfortunately, two months later, both Katie's parents were killed in an airship accident over Cape Cod.

When her sadistic uncle revealed the grim news, Katie collapsed. She lay as one already dead in her cold bed for three days, completely inconsolable, not that her uncle would ever comfort her. As Katie would later learn, the sly dog was too busy working with his solicitor to see that Katie's considerable inheritance came straight into his hands.

In the three years since they'd visited her mum's family, Aunt Agnes had taken a turn for the worse and been confined in a asylum. Katie endured life alone with her uncle and two servants. She hated Newport. She hated her uncle more. She felt like she'd been banished to hell; now that she was certain she'd be imprisoned here forever. Her uncle was all the family she had left, and *he* was a monster. *But what could she do?* There was her child to think of. She'd nowhere else to go. *Time to grow up, Katie, and stand on your own.*

LIKE CLOCKWORK

13

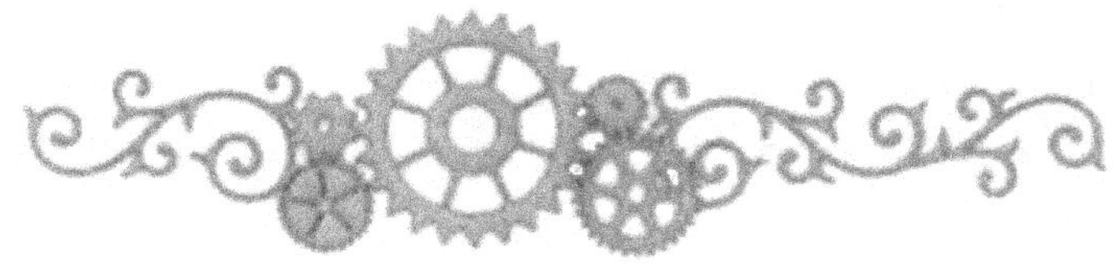

CHAPTER TWO

Wherein our stalwart down-trodden hero innocently blunders down a path toward further calamity.

The shark was making another pass, rubbing its sandpaper hide along Diego's flailing legs and then slowly undulating along Ned Wolfshadow's corpse for another helping of Native American flesh. Scott let his body go slack in the water, slowly drawing his long, muscular legs up toward his torso. The big White Tip started toward him. *He wanted to die.* Time and time again he'd wanted that, after losing his job and self-respect. After losing Katie. But not this way. Not being *eaten.*

Too bad there hadn't been a war to perish in. Die a hero's death. *Hero's death, my ass.* He'd run away. Chucked everything aside and run like a little drummer boy at his first battle. Bugger!

Eighteen-Ninety-Four. Sweeping a curl of wet, brown hair out of his eyes, Scott Wildethorne could hardly believe it'd been almost a year since he'd been kicked off the Boston Police force and gone to sea. A miserable year without a single word from Katie. Quitting Boston in disgrace and self-loathing, he'd hunted for a dangerous occupation—something requiring a certain amount of derring-do--in hopes of burning out his craving for the bottle along with the guilt from his tormented past.

Shipping out of New Bedford on a whaling bark, he'd worked himself up to second mate. He'd been relatively content with the dangerous work until they'd started talking about using the new bomb-lances on the poor beasts, and he'd suddenly lost his stomach for whaling. *Dead whale or a stove boat, my ass.*

Well, here he was hanging on the splintered remains of his stove boat. He'd been in charge. His boat. His men. Dammit, he'd lost three of them. Good stout comrades, every one. And now the shark was coming back for the rest. He'd brought company. Two other big buggers, nine foot Oceanic White Tips, not their smaller lazy namesakes he'd seen cruising off the reefs of Lahaina. His eyes rolled up in his head when he saw what was trailing them. An eighteen-foot Tiger. *They were so screwed.* These devils could swallow you whole. *Where the fuck was Flynn with the other boat?*

He'd thought to drown his shame, or take a chance on ending his miserable existence when a big bull whale smashed into his boat, but what chance did the dumb creature have when you shot it with a lance possessing an exploding head? And should the unfortunate beastie not die immediately but choose to flee by diving, the lance was fitted with a new-fangled tracking gizmo so you could just hang around waiting for it to bob to the surface, dead. *Oh yes, the clever clankertons' lance injected buoyant air into the wound so the whale's carcass was bound to rise. Where was the challenge in that?*

The damned joke was on him. With all their fancy new-fangled equipment, his boat had been the closest to the big bull sperm whale. And his had been the boat smashed to splinters when the old scarred bull hammered them with his flukes. He'd gotten the lance into the Sperm first; it was dead too. The whale rolled over on the men floundering in the water as it died. It filled the ocean with its blood, calling to the sharks like a full bottle to a drunk. And Scott knew all about how focused a drunk could get on a bottle of liquor.

Where was Flynn? Scott spied a small bobbing dot about a hundred yards away, growing larger. *Flynn's boat?* He heard one of the sharks going for Diego; knew there was nothing he could do to help the Cape Verdian. He decided it was Flynn's boat coming for them just about the time the eighteen-foot Tiger Shark joined in the feast. *Fuck me—this is no way to make a living. Or die.*

Five virile Yankee men went into the water with Scott. Good men, with sweethearts, wives and families waiting back in New Bedford for men who would never return. Good men; friends. When Flynn's boat finally pulled alongside, there were only two. Scott, the last in the water, was pulled to safety inches ahead of the Tiger Shark's greedy jaws. They'd recovered what they could of the other mens' bodies—precious little–hooked up the dead sperm whale and began the long row back to the whaleship. There was no hurry; even though the sea had grown choppy the fickle wind had died hours ago, eliminating the possibility of sailing. Scott sat glumly in the bow of the boat, an enraged, wounded lion, feeling the full weight of his mens' deaths on his broad shoulders. *Fuck this!* He'd made up his mind to leave the *Amazon* before they reached her bluff side. He had to see Katie, make sure she was all right. Make sure her encounter with that fiend in Boston had left no lasting damage. Even if she wanted nothing to do with him, he had to see her. It'd been a year; time enough for her anger and disgust to fade away. At least, he hoped it was. Inside, he was being eaten alive with worry and wonder. He might as well have let the damned Tiger Shark finish the job.

As the rowers ate up the last hundred yards between their whaleboat and the *Amazon,* a couple of odd moments jolted through Scott like harsh bolts of lightning. Unlike most whaleships, owned by stern, practical Yankees who knew how to squeeze a penny until it shrieked, *Amazon* had a proud Amazonian figurehead. Most whalers, owned or run by religious Protestants or Quakers settled for nothing fancier than a curled "fiddlehead". Not Ephraim Whipple. Captain Whipple had used his own coin to purchase a buxom figure of an Amazonian warrior in full armor and headdress, highly detailed and lovingly painted right down to her one naked breast. Scott had glimpsed the saucy figure a thousand times. The only problem was that this time, she wore Katie's face.

Just as disturbing was what he glimpsed aft, amidst the cluster of gawking boat crews and ship keepers. As the whaleboat pulled alongside and tied off to the whaler's bluff side, Scott would've sworn he saw a small, silent figure among the cat-calling crew, suddenly turn and walk away.

* * * *

He jumped ship in Lahaina, took the first inter-Island schooner to Honolulu and boarded an over-crowded zeppelin for the states almost before he got his land legs back.

Almost a year. Eleven months since he'd fucked up royally. All because of a cheap bottle of rotgut rum and soul-gnawing guilt riding his back like some blood-sucking vampyre. And, of course, the other thing.

There'd been a series of break-ins on his beat. He and Tim O'Rourke had caught a homeless Wampanoag man with a few of the stolen items in his possession. When they'd questioned him, the half-drunk Indian insisted he'd *found* the jewelry. So while Scott went to fetch the Paddy wagon, O'Rourke had beaten a confession out of Amos Littlefeather . When Scott returned with the police wagon and another peeler, he was too late to stop his partner from breaking the Wampanoag's arms.

Two days later, the battered Wampanoag was found hanging lifeless in his cell. How he'd managed to hang himself with two broken arms became the buzz of the precinct. Scott had his suspicions. A day after that, another pair of constables walked into the precinct leading a suspect who'd confessed to all the robberies. After his shift ended, Scott had started drinking.

A week later, an underpaid steamfitter working for the New England Boilerworks found his wife sitting in their front parlor with nothing covering her body but their next door neighbor. Roaring in enraged Italian, he'd hurled the nude, adulterous couple out into the North Boston street, and begun looking for his daughter, Theresa. Seizing his six-year old's hand, he'd caught the streetcar to the zeppelin park on the edge of Boston, and smuggled her aboard the evening dirigible to New York before the aerodrome police could catch him.

One of twenty Boston coppers dispatched to apprehend the man, Scott was the first one to corner Joe Conti and his daughter as the delayed *Zephyr's* propellers pushed it back to its mooring mast. Scott found the father and daughter backed against one of the dirigible's expansive observation windows, both obviously frantic to escape.

"Mr. Conti, listen to me, please. Sir, you're not in trouble here. You've committed no serious crime. Most of the boys on the force would've done the same thing, myself included. It's all a misunderstanding, easily cleared up." As he talked, Scott slowly eased his way closer. When he saw the threatening glare in Conti's eyes, he stopped. "Please, sir, just let your daughter go. Then you and I can have a nice talk."

It became quickly evident Mr. Conti's command of English was minimal at best. Scott wished one of the Italian-speaking cops involved in the search would show up. The guy was tottering on a razor's edge; it was clear he wasn't grasping anything Scott was saying and growing more frantic by the second. Scott got a creepy feeling things were going bad in a hurry.

"Look, sir, forget I'm a copper. Think of me as someone who wants to help you. You've gotten yourself in a bit of a pickle here, and I can help. But you've got to let Theresa go first. Your wife has admitted her guilt. Hell, in your shoes, I would've done the same thing."

"You are not in my Papa's shoes, Mr. Policeman."

God in Heaven, the kid spoke English.

"Look, Theresa, please tell your papa he's not in any trouble. I want to help him. He just needs to step away from the window and let me talk to him. Theresa—"

It happened so very fast. Not comprehending the command to release his terrified child, the hysterical father turned frantically pleading eyes toward Scott, seized his daughter around the waist and dove through the observation window. As she fell the little girl locked her sad brown eyes on Scott as if accusing him of giving them no other avenue of escape but death. She never cried out. Dropping his service revolver, an *Incapacitator* nine-shot, Scott fell to his knees as the doomed couple plummeted the three hundred feet to their deaths. Although each of the other Boston blue bottles arriving on the scene assured Scott he'd done all he could to prevent the tragedy, Scott felt he could have done more, done something differently, somehow saved their lives. Rather than let the torment eat him alive, he turned to the rum bottle for the comfort of oblivion.

The final straw had been Katie. While she was helping the Boston police in their pursuit of the Rude Ruffian, Scott had been introduced to Miss McBride. They'd worked together on numerous occasions, gradually becoming close friends. Among other things, she'd tried to help him deal with his guilt over the people he couldn't save. He'd never met anyone as sweet, lovely or compassionate before. In spite of the differences in their backgrounds, he thought they were well on their way to becoming far more than friends. He knew he'd fallen for her hook, line and sinker.

Then came that fateful night.

But that was all in the past. Now he was back ashore with money in his sea bag, a bit of a plan, and a blank slate on which to write in big, bold letters. He intended to approach Katie, beg her forgiveness if he had to, and make darned sure the life he hoped to achieve centered around her.

Trouble was, Katie wasn't in Boston. It seemed her parents had both been killed in an airship accident. Luckily, it looked like Katie hadn't been with her parents. None of the neighbors, footmen or maids he coerced into talking to him knew anything beyond the fact that one parlormaid noticed Miss McBride's sudden disappearance weeks *before* the tragic dirigible accident. Unfortunately, she had no idea where the rebellious young lady had disappeared to. Taken aback, but undaunted, Scott promised himself he *would* find her, once he'd taken care of some pressing family business.

* * * *

He caught the morning velocicoach from New Bedford to Fall River. The smoke-belching, horseless steam-carriage rocketed through Dartmouth and Westport, shaking up the passengers until their teeth rattled. As Scott consciously avoided the blatantly hungry stare of the young widow seated across from him, his tattooed hand strayed to the oft-folded correspondence hidden in his pocket.

He'd shipped out on the *Amazon* without telling any of his family or friends, thinking it best he just disappear. Sailing into 'Frisco for storm repairs before the last leg to the Alaskan whale fishery, he'd made time to contact his family and one or two friends, hoping to explain his actions. They already knew. His brother, Oliver, a successful owner of a Fall River cotton mill, told him there'd been inquiries into his whereabouts. When the full story of his embarrassing behavior in Boston and his dismissal from the police force surfaced, Scott's father had taken ill with a bout of Influenza. Within three weeks, he was dead. Because of the shame Scott had brought on the family, Oliver insisted their father had died of a broken heart.

The letter in Scott's pocket was from the family's solicitor. Among his many possessions, Thomas Wildethorne owned a half-forgotten, run-down shipwright enterprise in Newport, Rhode Island. Although the bulk of his estate had been left to Oliver and Scott's two sisters, Thomas left the near-defunct shipyard to Scott, should the ne'er-do-well ever cease running away and come home to face his demons.

Well, Scott had stopped running, and he intended to succeed with "Wildethorne Shipwrights". As long as he could remember, he'd loved anything dealing with boats and the sea, and most of his fondest memories of his father were their walks together along the seashore of Newport and Narragansett. His plans for the future however, were to raze the shipyard and turn it into the much more profitable trade of producing personal luxury airships for Newport's growing population of the ultra-wealthy.

* * * *

Cramming his ticket for the Fall River Line steamship's evening voyage into his jacket pocket, Scott swung himself aboard the electrified Main Street trolley, and grabbed hold of the first vacant brass pole. There was no way he was going to snatch a seat with so many ladies riding the streetcar downtown for shopping. Besides, he'd be getting off at South Main, close to the McWhirr store. A new suit, and shoes, not to mention a half dozen pairs of socks and gentleman's undergarments. Perhaps even a new derby. He intended to make himself presentable before boarding the luxurious steamer for Newport.

As the trolley screeched to a spark-spewing halt outside McWhirr Co., Scott prepared to disembark, almost bumping into the elderly matriarch descending ahead of him.

"Do be careful young man! Not all of us are in as much a hurry as you seem to be," scolded the stern-looking, well-dressed matron; her jiggling double-chins reminding Scott of a Christmas turkey's waddles. "Do have a care! Besides, enjoy the spectacle. It's not every day we see such a sight as this, thank the good Lord."

Following the direction of the portly matron's pointed finger, Scott watched a rather plump woman in her mid-thirties as she scuttled across the sidewalk and beat a path toward a hired-hackney. As she moved, the crowd parted, the way Scott imagined a romantic painter might portray the Red Sea drawing back from Moses or more likely shrieking young ladies retreating from rats. Apparently, the local crowd thought of this woman as some sort of pariah. On one side of the woman's tightly drawn back hair, Scott spied the oozing mess of a thrown egg. As the pinch-lipped crowd drew back from her in snubbing rejection, a few of the spectators drew back their hands to hurl more eggs. There seemed to be only one person willing to approach her. Stalking up close to the shunned woman, a sun-weathered gentleman angrily shook his fist in her face. Oddly, although he seemed to be raining blows on the outcast, she appeared to ignore him.

"Who is she, madam? And why does the crowd seem so repulsed by her presence? And who is the white-haired gentleman shaking his fist at her?"

"White-haired gentleman? Young man, we *all* despise her. Either you're a foreigner, or if you're the Yankee mariner I took you for, you've been on the other side of the globe! That's the infamous Lizzy Borden."

"I've been at sea for almost a year, madam. Before that . . . I'd heard of the case while working in Boston, but never saw an actual photograph of the woman."

"Let's stand over here, young man, out of the way and let these good people off the trolley." Grasping Scott's sleeve, she led him out of the mainstream flow of disembarking passengers. Though he towered over the woman, Scott allowed himself to be led to one side, like a bobbing skiff being towed into a backwater eddy by a stout steamer.

"Let's see now, if you remember, back in August of 'ninety-two, Miss Borden over there took an ax to her pa and stepmother. It was in all the newspapers. I'm sure even way up in Boston they have newspapers."

"Yes, madam. I've never had much time for reading the papers, but now that you mention it, I do recall seeing a small article in a paper while I was out in 'Frisco. No pictures though.""

"Well, anyway, I'm sure you've heard the ditty about giving her mother forty whacks. Unfortunately, those idiot jurors found her innocent, so we decent folk have to put up with the likes of her wandering our streets."

"So you believe she was guilty of the crimes, madam? You feel she murdered her parents?"

"Clara. Clara Wharton. Yes. Yes, I most surely do. Most of us do believe she butchered her father and stepmother. Probably some foolishness over money or a love affair. Some say she got off because she adored little animals and was a Sunday school teacher. Of course, that's sheer poppycock. There are as many rumors about Miss Borden as round rocks on Sakonnet's beach. I heard she had a lover her father disapproved of, and wanted money. Another woman, by God—a struggling actress of all things. Can you imagine such a disgusting, vile thing? It's an abomination in the eyes of Our Lord, is what it is!" She paused, very red in the face and began wheezing, leaning heavily on Scott's arm as she struggled to catch her breath. On a younger woman, he'd guess her corset was too tight, but Mrs. Wharton quite obviously wasn't wearing one. Trying to be patient, he mumbled soothing platitudes and gently led her to a nearby wrought-iron bench while he snuck a quick glance at his wrist chronometer. *Damn! Where was the day going?*

"Anyway, I'm a Captain's widow, and I can attest to many strange things bumping about on God's good earth, young man," she prattled on once she'd caught her breath. Her hand remained firmly on Scott's wrist, her arm tightly entwined with his. Scott was going nowhere soon. "Why, I remember my husband telling me the tale of that Nantucket whaleman of the *Essex*. Now, what did my Jeremy say his name was?"

"I believe he was Captain Pollard, Mrs. Wharton. I've heard the sad tale as well."

"Pollard—yes, that's the fiend's name. I knew you were a bright young sailor lad. Can you imagine eating your fellow man?"

"Y-yes. Actually I can almost imagine."

"That poor tike of a cabin boy. Rumor has it your Capt. Pollard once told a New Bedford news reporter: Know him; I ate him. Can you imagine? Then there was the case—"

"Thank you, Mrs. Wharton, for your time and delightful conversation, but I really must be going." Gently, but firmly, Scott extricated himself from Widow Wharton's clutches and slipped free as deftly as one of those fur seals he'd seen escaping White sharks off South Africa.

"Well I never! The impatience and rudeness of young people today," Clara huffed. "If you hadn't reminded me of my late husband in his sea-rig, I never would've wasted my breath."

Spying the men's clothier he wanted, Scott hurried down the crowded sidewalk, stealing a final look at the harried-looking Miss Borden as she ducked into the covered carriage. She probably was guilty of the murders if money was involved. *What was it the tabloids called the poisonous arsenic desperate and dissatisfied wives sometimes fed their husbands and fathers? Ah, yes, inheritance powders. Women, even ladies, were capable of so much more than their apparent frailty revealed. Take Miss McBride—God, he hadn't thought of her in at least an hour—sweet and fragile-looking as a flower, and yet she had the pluck to offer herself to the police as bait in order to trap the monster who'd murdered her friend.* Feeling a familiar pang of shame at his dismal part in that debacle, Scott mentally flogged himself. *Damn it! Am I ever going to be free of this devil? It feels like I've hung Coleridge's damned albatross around my neck.*

CHAPTER THREE

In which our dashing hero reveals he is a right stout fellow, brimming with plenty of manly vigor and plucky courage.

Early in the evening, as the white, side-wheeled steamship, *Priscilla*, got under way with only a few of her possible fifteen-hundred passengers strolling the decks, Scott Wildethorne checked his appearance in the gentlemen's water-closet mirror beneath flickering gaslights. The elegant white-clad steamer really did offer the very latest and most extravagant of luxury travel. The individual toilets in the gentlemens' water closet were *flush* toilets. Even the soap dispenser placed conveniently near the sink and gilded mirror offered *heated* shaving cream. As second mate working near *Amazon's* bow, Scott sometimes found himself forced to sit on one of the whaler's heads, opposite the bowsprit, and often experienced a slap of cold sea water on his naked bottom. This was so very much better.

He hadn't bothered with a cabin as he'd be disembarking in Newport, the Fall River Line steamer's first port of call. He paid a small fee to stow his bulging sea bag, and then headed out into the fresh air. With a final adjustment to his ascot, he shot his cuffs and headed aft toward the dining room.

Judging from the looks he kept getting, he didn't look too bad. Already a dozen young women had given him more than a lingering glance. One young blonde had virtually thrown herself into his arms.

Which is why later on, the cool, calm night found Scott walking outside *Priscilla's* grand salon arm-in-arm with Miss Sophia Bernstein of Westchester, New York. Raven-haired Miss Bernstein, attractive daughter of a prominent financier, seemed to be looking down her long nose at the honey blonde on Scott's other arm. Miss Phoebe Mullins, a giggling actress returning to New York after a successful Boston engagement appeared to be getting on Sophia's nerves. Scott just kept strolling forward, enjoying the tang of the salt air and the feel of a soft woman on each arm. Enjoying their giggling chatter, the swish of their elegant satin dresses and the subtle perfumed fragrance of his two companions, Scott realized how much he'd missed the company of women. It'd been a *long* year at sea.

If only it had been Kathleen McBride strolling by his side.

Lights from the steamer's forward cabins twinkled like starbursts and bounced across the evening waves. The strolling ménage stopped near *Priscilla's* port bow to enjoy the show and indulge in a little warm cuddling.

Suddenly, the steamer's searchlight flooded the sea ahead with blinding light, and the pilothouse steam-whistle tore the peaceful night apart with three, short, panicked blasts. Instinctively, Scott tore his eyes from his amorous female companions, straining to see what those in the wheelhouse had caught in the searchlight's glare.

A mere thirty yards to port, a local lobsterman was busily hauling up his pots. *More likely, they were stealing from someone else's pots,* the remnants of the policeman in Scott thought. *Hence the absence of running lights on the lobster scow.* The fool had brought along two young children, probably his own misbegotten spawn, their innocent faces caught in the searchlight's glare, their eyes full of fearful amazement as the huge steamer threatened to run them down. *What kind of parent brings along two innocent children, involving them in his life of crime?*

Scott knew what would happen moments before it did. Excusing himself from his lady friends, he quickly removed his expensive, new shoes, and climbed up on *Priscilla's* rail. Although the crew in the steamer's wheelhouse had seen the grimy lobster scow and had taken enough evasive action to miss the boat, the poacher would never escape *Priscilla's* impressive bow wave. Even as Scott dove overboard amidst the screams of both his companions, the massive wave hit the lobster boat and the poacher's little boy toppled into Narragansett Bay.

Priscilla, the flagship of the Fall River Line, never even slowed down. But some quick-thinking soul standing on the steamer's bridge hit the red button on the side of the binnacle and ejected two automated life rings. Even before they hit the surface of the cold night sea, each of the devices activated, producing a ring of bright greenish lights. In moments, Scott heard the life sphere's miniature steam engines rumble to life, initiating the throbbing squawking of tiny distress horns. In less than three minutes, each engine had built up a full head of steam—enough to power the dozen small heat jets suspended beneath each ring, enveloping the rescued person with vital warmth. Without it, Scott and the small boy would perish of hypothermia long before anyone plucked them from icy Narragansett Bay. Scott grabbed both life-rings, putting one around himself. Spying the decrepit lobster boat hovering nearby, Scott closed the distance between himself and the flailing youngster with a dozen quick strokes. He put a life ring around the boy before searching for the poacher's boat. Spying it, he spoke to the young boy gently, trying to dispel his fears and calm him before beginning the long swim to the poacher's wallowing boat

"It's all right, lad. Just try to relax and let me do the swimming. I'll tow you and have you back aboard your father's boat before you know it."

The terrified child looked at Scott with big brown eyes full of tears, and for a moment, Scott almost let him go. They were *her* eyes. Theresa Conti, the little girl from the zeppelin disaster. Shaking his head to clear the image from his mind and a mouthful of cold water from his lips, Scott took a firmer grip on the little boy's life ring. *Not this time. This time I <u>save</u> one.*

Reaching the starboard side of the lobster boat. Scott helped the young boy clamber back aboard as his ten-year-old sister yelled encouragement in Portuguese. . As Scott bobbed uncomfortably on the bay's surface, he realized he'd been wrong in two of his assumptions. Knowing the renegade lobsterman could never shed the cumbersome oilskin waders and coat in time to save his child, he was not overly surprised to realize the poacher had swathed his head in a muslin mask and light-gathering goggles. Yet, in spite of his disguise, a half-dozen of the poacher's snarled commands were enough to convince Scott *he* was in fact a woman. As for the lobsters stolen from another's traps, they *weren't* lobsters at all, unless edible-sized specimens of *Homarus americanus* came with blinking lights. So the lobsterwoman was a smuggler. But of *what*?

"Maria, be quiet. Wrap your brother up in the blanket and get under the tarp. Do it!" She waited a moment until her children were safely out of sight before turning her withering glare on Scott. "Mista, I am grateful for you saving my Manny, but you must let go my boat now. I am not letting you in."

"I understand. . . madam, but the water is starting to get pretty cold, and there are bad things swimming in the bay at night. For God's sake, I don't care what's under the tarp, just let me aboard."

"No! Back off now, or I use the gaff on youz! Go!"

Suddenly, a large leather and brass device the woman wore strapped over one worn gauntlet began to blink with a pulsating red light.

"Damn! The *Guarda Costeira* ! Get off! Get away from my boat! Now!" To emphasize her point, the yellow-goggled woman raised a weathered gaff and prepared to smash it down across Scott's clutching knuckles.

As mate aboard a New Bedford whaler, Scott was well able to understand the Portuguese woman's panicked declaration that the Coast Guard was coming. Deciding he'd rather bob for a bit in Narragansett Bay surrounded by marauding blue sharks than deal with five smashed knuckles, Scott let go of the boat's gunwale and back pedaled away from the scow. As he drifted with the current, he heard the mother giving orders to her two children in frantic Portuguese. Within seconds, the mystery woman's boat got up steam and chugged off into the murky night, looking like Charon's funereal ferry crossing the river Styx.

* * * *

"Are you sure *that's* the suit you want the fair ladies of Newport to be seeing you in, Scott?"

Scott was already beginning to peel off his soaked and slimy brown suit, realizing he'd badly split both of his jacket's underarms, not to mention the clinging seaweed and general stench of harbor water. Good thing Joshua had sent one of the boys to the Fall River Line's office to fetch his sea bag and belongings. It didn't hurt his ego to learn the steamer's bridge crew, as well as his female companions of the previous evening, were calling him a hero. The irate mother of the boy he'd saved certainly hadn't expressed the slightest syllable of gratitude.

Sluicing away the last of the bay's stink with two buckets of cold water, Scott carefully toweled off before opening his bulging sea bag for fresh clothes.

"Let's talk about the yard, Josh, while I dress. I saw two friendship sloops being rigged, another having her bottom coppered, and that big steam yacht with the hole in her bottom."

"*Nourmahal.* Billy Vanderbilt's boat. Supposedly he ran her aground off Beavertail light while he was busy below entertaining a couple of ladies. His Mrs. wasn't aboard at the time."

"So you're plugging this hole for the philandering Mr. Vanderbilt, while he plugs everything else. What else is happening around here?"

"Not much. Your father lost interest in the yard when your *mishap* occurred in Boston and you disappeared. Anyway, we could be taking orders for a lot more sloops, Scott. I know she isn't *Vigilant* or even that limey American Cup loser, *Valkyrie*, but our old *Rattlesnake* still turns a lot of heads when she flies into port with a bone in her teeth."

"Good." Slipping on his second boot, Scott hesitated a second before baring his soul to his childhood friend, and revealing his dream. "I want to get the yard bustling with work again, building ships."

"Great! That's such sweet music to my ears, Scottie Boy!"

"They'll be a different kind of ship, Josh. I want to build airships."

"Airships! Why?"

Standing up and stamping his booted foot against the floor's worn oak planking to settle his foot inside, Scott waited a second for his friend to swallow his bitter pill before trying to sweeten the moment. "I notice *Rattlesnake* appears ready to set sail. I'd like to take her up the bay around Rose Island and get reacquainted. When I come back, we can talk business."

"Might be a good thing. An hour at *Snake's* tiller might knock your mind back on course. Who the hell wants more zeppelins cluttering up our skies? Friendships are thee way for this yard to turn a tidy profit. Everybody loves them."

"The idle rich, Josh. Their own personal airships. Look, we'll talk. By the way, who owns that abandoned warehouse next door? We might want to make the owner an offer. We're going to need a bigger yard. Good thing they filled in the lagoon behind us, but we'll still need more room."

"Bigger? This one's mostly empty. You've got too much salt water sloshing around between your ears. Bigger—for Christ's sake, why?"

"To work on the airships' gas bags. Personalized monograms for our rich clients. I'm envisioning one-of-a-kind designs stenciled or painted on the airship's gas chambers. There's an awful lot of oil and railroad men setting up summer homes here and over on Jamestown. Lot of them got their own advertisements or trademarks they'd like to see on the side of a balloon. Not to mention family crests. With all this new wealth, lot of millionaires are tracing their roots back to family castles and titles in Europe. Some of them will want to see those on their balloon's gas bag. We'll talk about it later. By the way, who owns the land, Josh?"

"Retired cantankerous captain. Jebediah Coffin. Go for your sail, Scott. Dress warm, winds a mite stiff and it's a tad cool today. *Think* about this whim of yours!"

"So how do I find this Jebediah Coffin, Josh?"

"He and Thomas Clark were a couple of ship masters formed the Clark and Coffin Shipping Company. They both swallowed the anchor a couple years back. One of them succumbed to some disease he picked up in the tropics six months back. Elephant-something or other. Nasty business. I'm remembering it was Jeb Coffin who escaped the grave and was still alive last I heard. Heard he and a few others opened some sort of seamen's lending library."

"Think he's there? What's the address?"

"Go for your sail, Scott. When you come back, I'll tell you."

CHAPTER FOUR

Wherein our bumbling hero blunders into a wall of solid ice and receives his comeuppance.

True to his word, as soon as Scott made *Rattlesnake* secure to the wharf, Josh told his boss how to find old Capt. Coffin. Scott's sail aboard the friendship sloop had taken longer than he planned; the invigorating breeze off her patched mainsail and the caress of her worn locust wood tiller seduced him like a rekindled love affair. He'd flown up to Rose Island's lighthouse, then come about and sleuthed his way with long tacks back and forth across East Passage out past Fort Adams and Castle Hill light. Before he hit Beavertail, he spun the old girl around on her beamy bustle, and brought her screaming back to her mooring, chased by a following sea, and clutching a big white bone in her teeth. By the time he slipped the last mooring noose over Long Wharf's pilings, he was more determined than ever to buy the abandoned warehouse from Captain Coffin. With that additional space, maybe Wildethorne Ship Works could build airships *and* friendship sloops.

Scott chose to spend the rest of the morning securing Spartan yet comfortable lodging at the Sea Dog Inn run by jovial Abigail Goodwife. He replaced his ruined wardrobe before heading out to approach Captain Coffin with his proposal. Taking Farewell Street out of town, it was two in the afternoon before he pulled up in front of the impressive waterfront library in his hired hack.

Joshua had explained how several local sea captains leaving the sea to enjoy their old age ashore had pooled their resources to create the Seaman's Free Library. Long before Scott finished tying his nag to the huge anchor outside, he realized the retired blue-water captains had bought the brick and stone structure with more in mind than providing a source of free reading for local and visiting ships' crews. It was obvious at a glance the old Yankee captains saw the library and its grounds as a final resting place for their massed collections of treasures and curios from around the globe.

As he approached the dark brass doors of the library's main entrance with their ship's wheel knobs, he couldn't help admiring the two huge whale jawbones full of baleen hair framing the main doorway. Quietly entering the shadowy vestibule, he was overwhelmed by an impressive display of South Sea idolatry, weaponry, and artifacts keeping watch in smothering silence. Each item displayed had been meticulously labeled with an identifying title and description rendered in a concise hand-lettered font.

Everywhere he looked, the walls were festooned with marine paintings or photographs, many of which struck as deep into his memories as a well-aimed harpoon. There was a topsail schooner with storm damage to her masts from a rampaging typhoon. The next showed a New Bedford whaler, the *Acushnet* he thought, with a dead humpback alongside; the crew scampering over the whale's carcass, stripping it of its blubber amidst a churning sea of prowling sharks. In the distance, another whaleship approached. It looked remarkably like his *Amazon*. And there was the rowdy ceremony he remembered so well when crew members dressed as

Neptune and his bizarre entourage came aboard, the day their ship crossed the equator.

But the group portrait next to it caught and held his blue-eyed gaze. It was a grainy Eastman photograph of five dour-faced New England sea captains. Reading the legend of identification beneath the framed photo, Scott quickly found Captain Coffin. *Well, at least now he knew who he was looking for.*

Slipping deeper into the tomblike library, he passed a grouping of five massive ship's figureheads, carved and painted with varying degrees of expertise. Passing one of a huge, weathered raven with a homicidal gleam in his painted eye, he strode into the first hall of neatly-shelved books. Oddly, he thought he heard soft symphonic music playing on an Edison gramophone somewhere deeper in the library. Schubert? Vivaldi? It certainly wasn't Gilbert and Sullivan. *Maybe that was where he'd find Captain Jeb. Was the retired captain a music-lover, secretly indulging in his hoarded collection of Edison wax cylinders?*

Following the sound of Vivaldi's *Four Seasons*, Scott wound his way through aisles of worn books and treasured curios, his hesitant footfalls sounding to him like the thunderous rapping of Captain Ahab's peg leg in the silent library. Ironically, his eye caught sight of a copy of Melville's *Moby Dick* stacked next to several of his other, lesser known works. Just ahead, the narrow corridor of book-lined shelves opened up into the library's main reception area, revealing a massive librarian's desk, ornately carved, no doubt the prized property of some forgotten clipper ship's captain. Scott could still see the plates on the stout legs where it had been bolted to the ship's deck. It seemed abandoned.

About to call out Jebediah Coffin's name, Scott noticed movement down a side aisle. A woman, an assistant librarian or helper no doubt, stood poised high up on a sliding ladder, shelving a couple of books written by Jack London. Determined not to look up her skirt at the pair of shadowy calves just visible above her scruffy, high-buttoned shoes, Scott took in the frumpy, shapeless clothes in need of a rigid corset, dull russet hair pulled severely back and pinned into a prim bun, and the glint of round spectacles. *A spinster or widow willing to work for pennies, no doubt as plain as a Cape Cod dogfish.*

"Pardon me, Miss, I'm looking for Captain Jebediah Coffin."

His question burst through the library's tomb-like silence like a thunderclap.

The small woman froze on the ladder, obviously startled by an intruder's presence, and then turned around, instantly revealing she was far from a homely crone.

"Y-yes? How many I help . . . YOU!" she almost spit.

"My God—Miss McBride?"

"Well, by all the blessed saints, as I live and breathe, if it isn't Mr. Wildethorne, the very last person I expected or wanted to see in my library."

"Katie. By God, it is you, under all that . . . *stuff.* Of course it's me. It's Scott. You can't have forgotten my first name? And since when have you needed spectacles?"

"Mr. Wildethorne, because I'm a lady I'll ask you politely to leave immediately. I was about to close up. As for forgetting your first name, I'd quite forgotten *all* about you. I intend to keep it that way."

She removed her metal-framed spectacles with their round lenses, pinched the bridge of her delicate nose, and glared at him with the huge, beautiful blue eyes he knew so well. She was thinner than he remembered, and tired-looking. There was a definite air of sadness about her. And something else. A poorly-hidden, much more visceral emotion. Fear?

"As for my wearing spectacles, if you'd ever stopped wallowing in your self-pity long enough to acknowledge my existence, you'd already know I'm a bit myopic. Besides, the specs go with the job, and usually keep bothersome mashers like you from becoming a nuisance. Now, Mr. Wildethorne . . . please *go!* Don't come back!"

"It's just a little past two o'clock. Why do you have to close now? I'd like to talk with you, Katie."

"Miss McBride. Or Kathleen, if you must persist in being so vulgar and overly familiar."

"I remember a time when you tried desperately to hide your accent—so afraid the gentry would think you just another fresh-faced colleen from Ireland."

"I've changed, not that it's any of your business. I've grown up. Now, Mr. Wildethorne, if you'd be a gentleman for once and just leave."

"I'd like a chance to explain and. . . apologize."

"We've nothing to say to each other, Mr. Wildethorne. Please leave–I'm rather busy. You've taken up quite enough of my time. I must go—Nathaniel is waiting for me."

"Nathaniel? You've made a life for yourself then. You're married, or engaged?"

"Nathaniel is my *son*; no thanks to you. Giuseppe Puccini had me in his hands for almost an hour. He didn't murder me like the others, but he did *everything* else."

"Giuseppe Puccini?"

"The *Rude Ruffian*, you cog-brain! Of course, you didn't hang around long enough to find anything out. You jammed up the gears royally and then ran as fast as your precious whale oil." She hesitated, then just blurting it out, taking some small pleasure in seeing how her stabbing words hurt. "He ravished me, Scott. You weren't around like you were supposed to be, so the fiend had his way with me!"

"Oh God—I swear I didn't know. They said you were all right. I never would've left if I'd known. I would've—"

"Well you did leave. Not that it matters now. That's ancient history."

She placed the spectacles back on her face, pushed the thin wire bridge high on her nose, and turned to leave. "Look, I've got to go. I'm late for Nathan's feeding already. Please leave so I can lock up."

"But a son? A son by that rapist? Why—when, good Lord! Dammit. Katie. I-I . . . ."

"You? There was no you. No one to confide in, to help me out. *You* ran away, like the coward you are. Just get out!"

"Katie–I'm so sorry. You've got to believe me—I-I had no idea he'd-he'd actually done that to you."

"What-raped me, Scott? The fiend *raped* me. Don't be embarrassed. You can *say* the word. I've had to live with it for a whole year. Now, will you please leave!"

"All right, Katie. I'll go. I can see you're upset. By God, you've every right to be. I'm so sorry. Maybe we can talk later."

He stopped speaking when her hand flew to her hip defiantly. Turning, he slowly walked back the way he'd come. Then remembering his original purpose, he turned back. She was still watching him. For a fleeting moment, he thought he'd glimpsed regret in her eyes. For what, he wasn't sure. She'd obviously got a lot to regret these days. As he did. God- raped! He had to find a way to make things right with her. Even if they no longer had a prayer of being together, he silently vowed he'd try to help her out somehow. Seeing her about to speak, he said quickly, "I came looking for Captain Coffin. Is he about?"

"You missed him," she snapped. "You're too late, Mr. Wildethorne. Like you always are." She crossed her arms under her chest and began tapping the toe of one boot on the stone stairs. Scott could see she was seething.

"Missed him? Is he expected back soon?"

"Not in this lifetime. He's passed on."

"Jebediah's dead?"

"Got it on the first go-round. Amazing, Mr. Wildethorne. My uncle is dead. As you are, to *me,* Mr. Wildethorne. Oh why wouldn't you stay buried at sea? Now, please, if you'll just go!"

"I see your sharp Irish tongue hasn't grown dull, Katie."

Katie huffed in anger, pressing her lips together as if afraid her fury might come spewing out otherwise. She turned away, starting to walk back to her librarian's desk, then spun on one well-worn heel, glaring at him.

"Are you still here? Mr. Wildethorne, you're not wanted here. Go!"

Grumbling to himself, Scott decided he'd leave. *Damn.* He'd made a royal muddle of everything. He'd done quite enough damage for one day. As he turned to walk away, Katie placed two books of poetry on her desk and followed him as if to make sure he actually left this time.   Winding his way through the nautical exhibits, he finally saw the entrance and made a beeline for the front door. Katie followed, trailing him like a shark. He stopped at the door and said, "I can't believe Jebediah was your uncle."   When she didn't answer, but chose to merely point him on his way, Scott walked slowly down the crumbling brick stairs and began untying the half-hitch that held his nag. "Guess I struck out with Captain Coffin, but please, Katie, relent enough to let me see you safely home."

Katie glared at him as though he was a particularly disgusting roach she should crush under her boot's heel.

"Thank you, Mr. Wildethorne, but I live just down Gull Lane. Barely two blocks away.   Scott looked where she pointed; his face clouding with concern as he took in a discarded plague of All Hallows Eve decorations blowing down the cobblestone street, and lying sodden in the filthy gutter. As he looked at the poorly maintained tenements, he saw a variety of crude talismans nailed to the doors to ward off evil, clear indicators of the superstitious nature of the multi-ethnic neighborhood. He tried not to notice the yawning maws of countless shadowy alleyways, just waiting to snare the unwary.

"This neighborhood has quite a vile reputation; it's not safe here for a lady. This is the poorest part of town, Katie.

"That may be, Mr. Wildethorne, but thanks in part to you, I must call it *home*. Now, if you'll just do us both a favor and crawl back into your bottle."

CHAPTER FIVE

In which our fair damsel discovers a crack in her façade of ice, and begins to wonder if she's got it entirely right.

Kathleen tugged open her shirtwaist, and settled four-month old Nathaniel to her breast. Only when he was nestled safely in the crook of her arm and his little blond head began to suckle did she set her rocking chair in motion and begin humming the old Celtic lament that usually soothed them both.

Oh God, what a mess. Her Italian neighbor who watched over her precious babe while she worked at the library or tutored complained again that she wanted more money. Nat apparently had refused to sleep, crying for two hours after she'd left and upsetting Mrs. Rosellini's own toddlers. Katie looked around at her own dingy, draughty apartment, noticing the peeling, stained wallpaper, the rusty plumbing and the feeble coalfire barely keeping them warm. She took no pleasure this time in noticing the few nice things she'd rescued from the sale of her parents' home or her horrid uncle's mansion. *Clean.* That was all she could say of this dismal hovel she called home, and that was only because she mopped, swept and scrubbed as religiously as her mum had once attended daily Mass.

With tears shimmering in her eyes, she let her gaze shift around the crowded room as though she might find the answer to all her prayers hidden in the shadows. There was the emerald green blanket she was knitting for Mrs. Fitzpatrick, alongside the tam o'shanter she'd knitted for herself the week before. A true lady must master the most delicate of needlework, her mother used to squawk. *Needlework, my arse.* She knitted because this place was freezing. Unconsciously, her gaze fell to the blue blanket for Nat; she'd yet another three hours work tonight before it could be put into service helping to keep her son warm. Her rent didn't include the price of coal, and she refused to allow Nat to freeze. *Sometimes when the southwest wind blew in off Narragansett Bay it was just so cold!*

Her gaze settled on Teddy next. She'd brought her beloved bear with her from Boston when she'd first been banished to Newport and her hellish uncle's groping hands. She longed to hold the threadbare bear now. Curl up in her ice-cold brass bed, clutch Teddy to her chest and have herself a damned good cry.

Damn you, Scott Wildethorne. Why did you have to come back into my life? She brushed a wayward tress of freshly washed and ironed auburn hair out of her eyes, and wondered. *Was he trying to worm his way back into her life?*

As if sensing he was momentarily not the center of her universe, Nathan chose that moment to bite down in his eager sucking. Crying out more in surprise than pain, Katie looked down at her son. His angelic face gazed back at her in a blue-eyed innocence she knew too well.

"You devil," she scolded, though it was unclear to her at that moment which male she meant.

* * * *

It poured for three days; a cold late autumn rain, chilling to the soul. Yet for three days Katie McBride battled to hold onto her bumper-chute as she marched down the street to her place of employment, appearing to the world as the most devoted of librarians. Only a keen observer would've noticed that each day saw her with hair freshly washed, curled and pinned, and wearing a skirt and fancy shirtwaist more appropriate for her Sunday best. That same spy might've noted her frequent look toward the library's entrance and her occasional lingering gaze out of rain-streaked windows.

On the fourth day, the rain slackened and the temperature dropped. The sky overhead seemed to be brooding, the color of old slate tombstones. Ominous. Katie had just come in after retrieving Nathan from Mrs. Rosselli and was in the act of stoking up the coal fire when there was a strong knock on her door. Placing Nat in his crib, Katie hastened to open the door. Her landlady, Widow Dyer, stood in the doorway, her stern, disapproving prune of a face peeking out from the plain white dust cap she always wore, the only speck of color to this raven of a woman, though Mr. Dyer had been dead and buried for twenty-five years. Judging by the rumors she'd heard from Maria Rosselli and some of the other neighbors, Katie wondered if the grave had proved more inviting than his wife's bed, the poor man. She suspected it was the only way he could escape her nagging, disapproving tongue.

"When you've got your brat down for a mite, I'd like to see you upstairs, Miss McBride."

"Yes, Mrs. Dyer. I'll be up presently."

Katie nervously shut the door, afraid she already knew what her grumpy landlady wanted. The rent was slightly overdue. She'd just sold a quilt that day, but now the money would have to go to play the impatient Mrs. Dyer instead of long-suffering Maria Rosselli.

Washing her face in a porcelain basin of cold water, Katie toweled off, and pinned a few stray wisps of auburn hair into her Gibson girl bun before heading up to see Mrs. Dyer. She thought about changing her blouse—Nathaniel had spit up on her bodice as she was putting him down for a nap, but decided to keep the soiled shirtwaist on. *Wear something clean, and the old bat will think I've come into money and raise the rent.*

Mrs. Dyer opened her door on the first knock, almost as though she'd been hovering just the other side of the oak door and counting Katie's footsteps as she ascended.

"Took you long enough. Come in, come in. Don't be letting my heat out, young woman."

Katie scooted through the doorway like a frightened mouse. As soon as she was inside, she whirled about, her hands clasped at her sides as tightly balled fists.

"Mrs Dyer—about the rent—"

"This ain't that, though I expect to have it in my hands by week's end. Think I've been mighty generous letting it lag as I have. Seems like the Christian thing to do, seeing as to your circumstances. No, this is about *that*," she said, pointing to a bag of groceries sitting on her dining room table. Man delivered it from Garibaldi's Market. Wanted to leave it in the hall downstairs— well I wouldn't have it. You know how long free food would last in this neighborhood. So I had him bring it up here."

"It's for me? I don't understand. Who would be sending me a gift?"

"You got a fancy man or somebody sweet on you? I don't want any trouble with men in this building. Mr. Briggs is the only exception. *He* pays his rent."

"No. No fancy man as you put it. No one. Nathan is the only man in my life."

"Well, be that as it may, take your groceries. They're cluttering up my table."

Katie glanced inside the open bag, noting that Mrs. Dyer had no problem snooping and wondered if she'd pilfered anything. Grasping each end of the drawstring, she cinched up the bag, while she tried to gauge her reaction to the milk, bread and fresh vegetables she had seen inside. She absently thanked Mrs. Dyer and picked her way carefully down the rickety stairs, her mind lost in the turmoil of wondering who'd been so kind.

As she put away the last of the groceries, she determined that there was no card or hint of her benefactor inside. Archibald Briggs was away, so it wasn't him--t*hank God.* But *who?* She was used to men's lascivious stares, and was no stranger to the trinkets and scrawled romantic notes of lovesick admirers. *But groceries?* This person *knew* her. *Knew what she needed.* It took her a long time to fall asleep that night; wondering who her benefactor was.

Afraid that she knew.

Four days later she came home to a similar surprise. This time, Mrs. Dyer had unlocked her door and left the groceries inside with a note demanding her rent. Once again, Katie had trouble sleeping, though this time she knew who'd sent the groceries.

How dare he!

*****

The next day the sky was the color of old lead again. Old man weather added the growl of thunder to the soaking rain. Katie sneezed and then continued preparing her son for the neighbor woman. It was no time for her to fight off a case of the sniffles. Firm knocking penetrated her next sneeze. Already harried in the extreme, she jumped. Annoyance added a jerk to the pull she applied to the doorknob.

God in Heaven, it was him.

If he'd been a smaller man she might not have recognized who was hiding behind all those precariously grasped and bulging sealskin bags—though the water proof bags were a good clue. Then again, she had a pretty good hunch before she opened her door with its peeling paint and rusted clockwork lock. She'd been half-dreading his return for three rainy days. Now he'd arrived dramatically in the middle of a thunderstorm.

"I thought we had an understanding, Mr. Wildethorne, that you wouldn't pester me ever again!"

Perhaps it was the mountain of gifts he brought, bribery no doubt, but just a glimpse into the top of each sack he opened on the floor near her feet revealed that each was stuffed with baby items she could never afford.

How dare he assume! But of course any fool could tell if she had this kind of spending money, she would move to a nicer, safer part of the city. Damn him! Didn't she feel inadequate enough already? These things would make her little tike warmer, healthier, and happier. They would make her life easier.

If only she could accept!

Perhaps it was the humble face he wore, those sky blue eyes she'd always been unable to resist, so full of repentance, regret and perhaps even a touch of sorrow. More likely it was the wind-driven rain sheeting in from the bay. She could see he was getting drenched as he stood there waiting to be invited in. Also uninvited, the swirling rain blew past him and into her open doorway. In seconds it'd be freezing inside. *Damn.* She never could abide seeing even the meanest slum dog half drowned and miserable.

She stepped back and allowed him to angle around the sacks to enter.

But only as far as her front hall, which in her run-down tenement meant right into her parlor.

"Well, don't just stand there like a drowned rat. Get out of that wet jacket. And don't you go thinking this changes anything, Scott Wildethorne! I wouldn't leave my worst enemy out there in this southwester if I could help it."

"Does this mean I'm not, Katie?"

"Not what? And please do me the courtesy of addressing me as Miss McBride."

"Your worst enemy . . . Miss McBride."

"You never were my enemy, Mr. Wildethorne. You know that. You're just the sorry-assed drunk who abandoned me when I needed you most. Then because of your shame, you took off without a word, not even bothering to find out if I'd lived or perished."

"I knew. I made sure I knew--though of course I didn't know all of it. Nobody bothered to tell me you'd been ravished. That you were pregnant. I wish I could change what happened, what I did and didn't do. But I've changed. I haven't touched a drop since the day I went to sea. I'm not the same man. I'm ashamed of what I did, how I failed you. I'm here partly because I want your forgiveness; I *need* your forgiveness, Katie."

"So now I'm responsible for your needs? One I'm sorry and that's supposed to make it all right? What about *my* shame, Scott Wildethorne? You wallowed in drunken self-pity while my life was destroyed by a monster! Because of you, I'm considered a ruined woman. All because I was taken in by your pretty eyes and soft words. Well, never again, Scott! I learned the hard way what men are really like. It was a hard, brutal lesson, but I survived.

You're not the only one who's changed! I'm doing perfectly fine standing on my own two feet now." She paused, splaying her hand beneath her throat as she struggled to catch her breath, and keep the tremble of erupting emotion out of her voice. From her tiny bedroom she could hear Nathaniel begin to move around in his crib. "I should ask you to leave right now, rain or not. All these things—you thought to *bribe* me? You think so little of my moral fiber you think I can be *bought* like a common whore! What makes you think I need or want gifts from you? What is it you really want, Scott?"

"Forgiveness. But as I see that's impossible, there is something else."

"What? Stop wasting my time and just tell me."

"Joshua Steele told me you came looking for me two weeks after I left, and that you arrived in a hired brougham—so I don't suppose your parents approved. All he knew about you after that was that he heard you moved in with some cantankerous old uncle at Blackbriars out on Devil's Keep. He didn't say it was Jebidiah Coffin."

When Katie remained silent, he added, "I heard about your parents. I'm so sorry for that, Katie. I should've been here for you. Rumor has it your father was in debt and died without a will. The house and everything else went to paying off the debt. You got nothing."

Katie saw no reason to tell him the rumor, like so much else in her life, had got twisted. Father's debt had been relatively small. The truth was that somehow Mother had convinced Father to will everything, including her care to Uncle Jebediah. *At least that's what she'd been told when the solicitor Uncle Jeb had hired read the will. It also stipulated that in the event of her parents' deaths, Uncle Jebediah would have complete control of her inheritance and could dole it out as he saw fit.* She saw no reason to correct Scott's misinformation. She saw no need to tell him *anything.*

"That's none of your concern, Mr. Wildethorne."

"No, maybe it's not. But why are you living *here*, Katie when you could be comfortable in your uncle's house? Surely, as his sole surviving heir you're entitled to quite an inheritance? From what little I've heard you virtually took care of him day and night during his last months. You've certainly earned whatever he chose to leave you."

"It's Miss McBride or Kathleen at least. And what I did for Uncle Jeb is none of your business. You're far too familiar, Mr. Wildethorne. Perhaps we were close at one time, sir, but you threw that privilege away, didn't you? You're supposed to be telling me what it is *you* want, not asking so many personal questions. Do get on with it, or leave."

She watched her rebuke push a slump into his broad shoulders. He reached up to rake his fingers through his hair in an attempt to keep the damp curl that persisted in falling over his eye from obscuring his vision. *Why did she envy him that nonchalant gesture?*

"Well, since you've cut yourself off from your uncle's money, and seem determined to live in this slum, I thought the least I could do to begin making amends was to bring along a few useful items. Diapers, a couple warm outfits, a rattle and this." He held out a bar of dark chocolate he'd kept wrapped separately. "Go ahead—Miss McBride. Take it. I promise, it's not a bribe."

Katie hadn't meant to. In fact, her brain had denied the kindness. Her love of chocolate, however, the longevity of that delight, the fading memory of the last taste she'd enjoyed, overruled her better sense. Gingerly, she reached out and took the chocolate bar from his hand like a nervous temple monkey seizing fruit, fearful it might be withdrawn. Or a trap. She noticed the wrapping paper. It even came from her favorite candy shop in Boston, Weiz Confections. *So, he had gone to Boston first. Perhaps looking for her?* Unable to resist the lure of the rich treat, she slowly unwrapped it, savoring the engulfing aroma of rich, dark chocolate. Then, quickly, with an inward squeal of delight, she broke off a piece and popped it between her lips, letting the oily, bittersweet candy glide across her tongue, thrilling her taste buds and filling her whole mouth with delight. *Damn him.* Her eyes drifted shut as she savored the rare moment.

"See, I *do* remember some things, Katie. Especially the ones you like."

Her eyes snapped open, the spell broken. "Apparently not my proper name . . . *Kathleen.* So . . . Mr. Wildethorne," she said between small flicks of her tongue against the inside of her teeth so as not to miss a single drop of flavor," what exactly is it you'd be wanting . . . besides forgiveness?"

Scott hung his head at her stinging rebuke, obviously frustrated by the cold wall of ice she kept throwing up in front of him.

Too bad. I can't let you try to dimple your way back into my heart.

His hands fidgeting with the brim of his soggy derby. He placed it on the floor, next to a small nicked table cluttered with knitting. Gazing at the threadbare stuffed chair closest to him, he asked if he might sit for a minute so they could talk.

Katie nodded, and he sat, narrowly missing the broken spring she'd forgotten about. *Of course he could sit. She, at least, had some idea of proper behavior. Unwanted or not, he was a guest.*

"Well, I thought maybe-oh—I can hear your baby, Nathaniel, getting restless in the other room. Wouldn't you prefer to go to him first; maybe bring him out here to be with you while we talk?"

"No! He'll be fine for a few minutes more. If you're so concerned about my son, please just get to the point, and *go*, Mr. Wildethorne."

****

Shaking his head in reluctant acceptance, he told her as sole benefactor of her uncle's holdings, she could get him out of her hair forever by selling him the waterfront warehouse. He was prepared to explain why, telling her about expanding the shipyard, and hopefully enthralling her with his plans to build small dirigibles and airships for the wealthy. He never got the chance. Her firm NO, and the defiant flick of her skirts as she rushed to the doorway crushed his hopes for reconciliation.

* * * *

A few days later, Mrs. Rosselli gave her half a loaf of two-day old garlic bread wrapped in a stained newspaper—making her feel guilty for wondering if the rather bristly old woman had stolen groceries from her gifted bag. When Katie unwrapped the aromatic bread, and smoothed out the wrapper so she could cut herself a slice, two news articles jumped out at her. She avoided the first, which spoke of another gristly murder in lurid detail, but she devoured the second along with her buttered slice of bread, quickly reading it a second and third time. *Perhaps he had changed. Had she been too harsh on him?* He had offered to purchase the warehouse, and God knew she could use the money. Maybe move to a warmer, *safer* tenement.

Funny, she'd been so busy trying to put bread on the table and coal in the stove she'd never given a second thought to her uncle's other holdings. She'd been so quick to condemn any thought of dealing with that dungeon her vile uncle called home she'd never even considered he might own other properties. Of course, she couldn't sell her uncle's mansion without adhering to certain unpalatable conditions, but why not sell the warehouse? Sell it and be done with Mr. Wildethorne once and for all.

That was what she wanted, wasn't it?

LIKE CLOCKWORK

55

CHAPTER SIX

Wherein Miss McBride sets down firm rules and reveals tantalizing secrets.

Two days later, Scott sat in the shipyard's tiny office studying plans and trying to conjure a way to build both sloops and airships within the yard's restrictive confines. He'd just thrown another chunk of scrap oak in the wood-burning stove and was trying to work amidst the snap and crackle of bursting knots from an earlier log of white pine. Joshua Steele knocked and entered, declaring a determined young lady had arrived in a hired cab and was demanding to speak with Scott. Scott chuckled, wondering aloud if one of his crew had slipped out of Madame Fong's pleasure palace without paying again. Josh was about to assure him this was no irate strumpet but a real lady when the fuming spitfire stormed into the crowded office behind him.

"How dare you! Scott Wildethorne, how *dare* you do this to me again?"

"Ah . . . Boss, I think I'll go see the men don't install Mr. Vanderbilt's new brass steam whistle upside down or something." Josh was out through the slamming door quicker than a nervous mouse.

"Thanks, Josh." Turning to his unexpected guest, Scott gave Katie McBride a surprised reassessment, noticing everything from her obviously new feathered top hat to her mud-spattered high-heeled boots. There'd been an icy cold rain the night before, and though it'd warmed, the boatyard was still muddy. Quite wisely, the woman had used the wide ribbons extending from the bottom of her corset to brail up the hem of her ground-kissing skirt, much as one would take a reef in a sail. That single action had gone a long way to keeping most of the muck off the previously trailing hem of her skirt.

"Now, Miss McBride . . . how dare I *what*? After our last meeting, I hardly expected to see you again, much less to see you strolling through my boatyard."

"You know very well what I mean. You've gone and turned my whole world upside down. Again."

"Sorry. I don't know when I could have found time to do all that. I'm rather busy trying to find room to squeeze in everything I need to build now that you've refused to sell me your uncle's warehouse." He bit his lip, trying desperately to control his own rising adrenaline. Before he began again, he allowed himself another long lingering drink of the angry woman before him. *What had she done with her hair? Kathleen McBride really had matured into a lovely woman.* "As for turning your world upside down, I have no idea what you're talking about."

She took a deep breath and visibly calmed herself. In a much quieter tone, though still understandable despite the whirring, grinding, bangs, clanks, yelling of orders and generally organized chaos from the yard, she said, "Those gifts you brought were generous, thoughtful, even though I knew they were nothing but bald-faced bribes. Still, they were . . . needed, and useful. Thank you."

"It's little enough, after what I did to you. After the way I, after I. Oh, well, my sister picked those out."

"Your sister. You never—we never talked about your family."

"Yeah, well with what's left of the Wildethorne *dynasty*. I've managed to hold on to one sister who hasn't completely disowned me. She was full of questions, of course, but finally she did agree to do some shopping for me."

"Did she pick out my new topper as well?"

"You don't like it." He sighed. For some reason he had known it would look perky and yet sophisticated on her. To his eyes, it did just that. With heartfelt regret at her disappointment, he said, "I wondered if it was a bit too flashy. I'm afraid I'm responsible for that blunder."

"No, no . . . I *love* it. It's not that. Wait. *You* picked this out?"

"Yes," he said softly, deciding not to mention how the color picked up the blue in her eyes. *Fiery* blue.

"Oh," she said simply. Her expression shifted. Squaring her shoulders, her features again registered a mood shift. Katie had gone from angry to defiant and then on to hurt, her eyes shining with unshed tears.

But she wasn't through, and like a warming teapot, her indignation bubbled to the surface again. From her beaded reticule she pulled a torn page of newsprint, and quickly unfolded it atop the sprawled blueprints on his desk. "Most importantly, you forgot to mention this."

Scott stared at the crumpled page from the *Newport Daily News*, quickly scanning the columns in search of what had so roused this steam-kettle's whistle.

"Which article, Miss McBride? The one on President Cleveland? Or this one on the discovery of another body on Easton's Beach?" He thought it best he be considerate of the young woman's more delicate sensitivities and not mention the one story in the *Daily News* that had caught his attention—that of a young parlor maid whose body had been found splayed across the gravestones of the old burying ground south of the North Baptist church for all to see. The decomposing woman's body had been split open and displayed on the weathered slate stones like some grotesque automaton left- over from a tasteless All Hallows Eve prank. *Yeah—he'd keep quiet on that one. He was already in enough trouble.*

One of Newport's finest undertakers assured the police she'd been dead for at least a week, somehow over-looked in the everyday hustle and bustle of the busy seaport. The story disturbed him greatly. He'd recognized the murdered maid's face. He'd seen her, recently, hurrying down Thames Street as though all hell was after her.

"I think we can dispense with the Miss McBride now, Scott. You know my Christian name. You may call me Kathleen. And you know very well which article I'm referring to! This one, describing an act of supreme heroism on the steamship *Priscilla*. It's talking about you, Scott. This is *you* with these two ladies, isn't it?" She repeatedly tapped the grainy photo with one finger of her dove gray glove.

Jack didn't have to read the article or see the picture someone had snapped of him walking arm in arm with two lady friends aboard *Priscilla*. He could vividly remember every moment, the soft feel of Phoebe's bosom brushing against him, the not so subtle scent of her perfume, and the icy, needle-like bite of the night ocean. Irrationally, he wished Katie hadn't seen him happily enjoying the company of those two women.

"I might've lent some small aid—well, *somebody* had to do something! The kid was looking right at me, Katie. He was going to die!"

Kathleen ignored his use of the overly familiar Katie instead of her proper Christian name this once. He sighed in relief. Perhaps her fury was finally cooling.

"It was the act of a selfless hero. You told me you'd changed. I chose not to believe you, but anyone who does what you did, who knowingly chooses to jump into the bay's icy cold water to save a little boy he doesn't know can't be a falling down drunk, and certainly is no coward." She stopped, placed one slim gloved hand on his forearm and said softly, "I've decided to sell my warehouse. You were right this once. I do need to think of my son's safety. With the money from this sale, I should be able to move us both into a much better neighborhood."

"You can't know how good that makes me feel to hear you say that, Katie. Of course I'd be delighted with the sale, but I've been worried about you and the boy."

"Kathleen, please use my proper Christian name. Katie makes me sound like a bar maid."

"Kathleen, then. This sale will benefit us both. Your son and you, of course, but also the men and their families who work for me. Shipbuilding is a very seasonal occupation. Now they'll be able to work indoors during the winter months, and be able to build my airships as well as friendship sloops."

"Airships? You always were a dreamer, Mr. Wildethorne."

"Scott, please, Katie—Kathleen. Call me Scott."

"Mr. Wildethorne, don't overstep the bounds of proper society. This is a business venture. Nothing more. I intend to drive a very hard bargain for my warehouse."

"As well you should. I intend to be generous."

"Why? I'd think you'd be the sort to take advantage of me, a poor, defenseless woman."

Scott rose from behind his desk and rounded its corner to stand beside her. He tried to take her hands, a friendly gesture to close the deal. She flinched away, as though his touch might burn her. Surprised, he rocked backward, leaning against his over-loaded desk as if she'd physically struck him.

"Is that how you see me, Katie? A minute ago you were calling me a hero."

"With *other* people, Mr. Wildethorne. I haven't forgiven you. I'm not sure I can. In fact, I'm positive I shouldn't…for my own good."

* * * *

Kathleen's mind raced, churning with chaotic thoughts, spewing out words without inner approval. *What did she really think? Was this purely a business visit?* Deep inside, was there a glimmer of hope that Scott would rise to the occasion and finally *be* her hero? *Was this what she wanted?*

"So where do we go from here, Katie?"

"Kathleen, please. And I haven't said anything about a "we" going anywhere. For now it should be enough that I'm trying to believe you, to understand how and why you made some of your past choices. Beyond this business together, there is no *we*."

"Well, it would seem we're about concluded here then. What did you wish to receive for the sale of this warehouse?"

"I was thinking four hundred dollars. To be delivered, in cash, to me at the library. By special courier. You are not to come."

"Four hundred. In cash." He made a point of hesitating too, as if counting to two hundred before answering. "No."

"No?" She was shocked. Her long fingers fluttering to her throat, toying with the worn lace of her high collar. "I believe that's quite a fair price, Mr. Wildethorne."

"My offer is for five hundred. In cash, in your hands within a week. By your request, I shall not deliver it, but it will arrive, delivered to your hand at the library."

"Five hundred?"

"Yes. Is that satisfactory, Miss McBride?"

"And you agree I will not have to deal with you after this?"

"Yes. On one condition of my own."

"Which is, sir?" she said, suddenly wary.

"Have luncheon with me to seal the bargain. It's well past noon and I'm famished. I imagine you are as well. Very respectable, public place. Close by. One hour of your time, no more."

"Of course not–" She'd been about to refuse, but then recalled he'd said she'd have her money within a week. Until then, she was still quite without funds. She'd less than three silver dollars in her reticule, and there was still the cab fare home, not to mention Mrs. Rosselli.

"All right. As long as I approve of the restaurant, and you behave like a perfect gentleman. One hour. After that, our business shall be concluded, and I can return to my son."

"Sounds fair enough."

"One more thing. A condition of my own. I will not see you again. We go our separate ways, lead our separate lives. No more little gifts. No contact whatsoever. Agreed?"

Maybe she was a keen business woman after all. This was not going at all the way Scott had hoped. *What could he do?* If he refused, she'd walk out. *He wanted the warehouse. He wanted Katie too, but–*

"I agree. No more contact. *For now.* Shall we go?"

Wayne Tripp

LIKE CLOCKWORK

CHAPTER SEVEN

Strictly Business

Scott had been truthful, a perfect gentleman. The restaurant he picked was called *The Laughing Gull,* a large stone and wood edifice overlooking Narragansett Bay, with an airy open dining room almost filled to capacity with well-dressed, polite diners carrying on quiet conversations and more intent on the splendid luncheon before them than ogling the couple being escorted to a table with an excellent view of the bay. Scott held out a chair for Katie, and then took one opposite her, a good table-width away.

Katie unpinned her hat and placed it on the vacant chair next to her. A few deft movements and pins later, she'd set her hair to right, and began removing her coat. It was toasty warm in the restaurant, so unlike her own place.

"Might a gentleman be permitted to say how lovely you look, Miss McBride?"

"What? Certainly not. I've accepted your invitation strictly as part of a business arrangement. Kindly refrain from trying to turn this into anything personal."

She noticed Scott was still watching her. How could she not? His acute observation of her every move and feature was definitely not a lascivious leer. It felt as if he were memorizing every contour and gesture, as though he might never see her again. And why shouldn't he? That's what she'd told him, wasn't it? That's what she wanted. This was going to be more difficult than she'd imagined. Katie had to do something to break the mood, to distract him. To distract herself from the wrong direction her thoughts were taking her. After all, this was strictly business. It could never be anything more. For a fleeting moment, she allowed herself the fancy that he was being truthful, that he's grown up, matured, realized what a fool he'd been to run away and leave her behind. But no, she couldn't take any chances with her darling little cherub. He was her responsibility and she, for one, did not run away from her responsibilities. Not that she wanted to. He was the best thing that had ever happened to her. No matter what.

"So, do you dine here often, Mr. Wildethorne?"

At that moment, the waiter suddenly appeared, rescuing her briefly, allowing her to collect her thoughts. He was a short, sparse man, with well-pomaded hair parted down the middle and a huge handlebar mustache that dominated his olive-toned face. *His* gaze, when it settled on Katie, was lascivious.

"Good afternoon, mademoiselle, sir. My name, it is Marcel I shall be your server. May I start you both off with a something to drink?" As he spoke, he gently placed a large menu in Katie's gloved hand and handed one across the table to Scott. Katie opened the menu and realized most of the fancy script was blurry. Reaching for her reticule, she caught the hovering waiter staring at her bosom. Flustered, Katie fumbled in her reticule for her spectacles. When she looked up, the waiter was taking a keen interest in the ornate tin ceiling. Obviously, he was aware she'd seen him. *Men. They could be such vulgar animals. He reminded her of...no, she wasn't going to think about that, not ever again.* She put on her spectacles and cleared her throat. Immediately,

Marcel became the professional waiter once again. "Ah—something to a drink, then? A nice wine, coffee or tea for mademoiselle perhaps, and an ale or beer for the gentleman?"

"I'd like a nice cup of tea, please," Katie replied in her most lady-like manner, her wide blue eyes narrowing as she stared at the waiter, warning him his attentions were unwelcome.

Pretending not to notice, he seamlessly said, "And for you, sir?"

"You will first tone down your over attentiveness to the lady, and please don't insult either of us by pretending you don't know what I'm referring to. After that, I'd kill for a sarsaparilla. Bring me a large one, please."

"Of course, sir. My deepest apologies. Forgive me. One steaming cup of our very finest tea for da lady, and one sarsaparilla carbonated beverage for the gentleman. Coming right up." With a swish of crisp white apron and bouncing mustachios, Marcel turned on his heel and disappeared.

"Did he make you feel too uncomfortable to dine, Kathleen? I can assure you, the food here will go a long way toward making up for his crudeness."

Obviously Scott had been watching and seen the waiter ogling her. His deft dealing with the man was impressive. If only he had come to her rescue in the same manner a year ago. His choice of sarsaparilla over beer hadn't gone unappreciated either. The old Scott wouldn't have hesitated a minute to order a brew.

"A silver dollar for your thoughts, Kathleen."

"What?" Embarrassed, and annoyed a man had made her feel that way, Katie had begun perusing the over-sized menu, hoping to hide until the rosy blush left in her cheeks.

"You seem to be deep in thought." He chuckled, sending an undesired thrill through Katie's heart.

It felt almost like old times, when he used to say the wittiest things and then share the most heartwarming laughter with her. How she'd missed the musical sound of his laughter.

"Having second thoughts about a few of your restrictions, Kathleen?"

"Certainly not," she snapped, louder than she'd intended. Her cheeks felt as if they were on fire. "I was merely beginning to review the menu and make a few choices."

"Order anything you like, Kathleen, but if I may be so bold, the homemade New England clam chowder is the best I've ever had."

"Really. Do you come here often, Mr. Wildethorne?" Looking up from reading a description of fillet of sole, she caught the eye of an attractive brunette at the next table staring at Scott with blatant appraisal.

"Once a week. Special days."

"And do you bring your special . . . lady friends with you?"

"I have no lady friends, Katie."

Before she could think of a cutting remark, their waiter reappeared with their drinks. Instead of leaving, he let the empty drink tray flop against the front of his shin to chest apron and withdrew a small pad and nub of pencil.

"Are we ready to place the order? Or would you like a few more minutes?"

"I believe I'll have the New England clam chowder to start," Katie said, seizing the lead. "Followed by the Atlantic salmon, a baked potato and your fresh-cut green beans." Katie hesitated, noticing the waiter's eyes this time were focused somewhere over her head. Across the table, Scott was watching, scowling at the man. "Oh, and if you could bring a basket of hot muffins and butter, that would be appreciated too."

"Very good, mademoiselle. And for you, sir?"

Appearing distracted, Scott ordered, choosing entrees and companion dishes that didn't really complement one another.

"You might've ordered the lobster. It's excellent here, as fresh as it comes. I recall in Boston you talked about having it at home—oh, I'm sorry. That was thoughtless of me."

"I'd only indulge in a steamed lobster dinner if I was in the company of a gentleman suitor. Since you've proven to be neither, I chose the fish dish. Besides, I *like* salmon."

"Wise choice then," came his curt reply, far from what she'd expected. Following his gaze which was neither on her breasts or face, she saw him scowling at a table across the way where two gentlemen and a lady were enjoying the remnants of their meal and having a lively conversation.

"Do you know them, Mr. Wildethorne? Care to share a few words with them? I'll dismiss you."

"Woman at that able. Trying to get my attention. Saying something I couldn't hear. Now she's just staring."

"Staring at you? Who, Mr. Wildethorne? Who's staring at you?"

"The blonde next to the mutton-chopped gentleman with the pince-nez. Look, she's gesturing again. Surely you see—"

Finished with their meal and conversation the lady and gentlemen rose, blocking Katie's view of anyone else seated at their table. When they turned to leave, the chairs around the table were empty.

"She's gone. Disappeared. But she was there."

"I see no one, Mr. Wildethorne. Perhaps, you should have had that beer. Or perhaps you've already had one?" She hadn't smelt the slightest hint of alcohol, but she couldn't resist the invitation to stick in her knife and give it a twist. The man had *ruined* her life, and here she was struggling to retain her anger.

"I told you I haven't touched a drop since Boston. I wasn't lying. Please, Kathleen, you must believe me. I was probably mistaken. I've been putting in a lot of extra hours at the shipyard. Probably seeing things, so over-tired."

The waiter chose that moment to show up with their luncheon, saving Katie from showing any sympathy for Scott. Once he left, the couple set to, enjoying their food as well as the view and doing their best to avoid any more awkward conversation.

Raising a forkful of sea bass to his lips, Scott looked across at his silently munching companion to notice her replacing the pocket watch she wore suspended on a rose ribbon from her pale blue bolero jacket.

"I gather my time has about run its course, Katie. They offer the most delicious of desserts here. Can I possibly delay your departure by tempting you with something in chocolate?"

"I couldn't possibly. I have a young son waiting for me. I thank you for luncheon, Mr. Wildethorne. It was delicious. But I'm afraid I must decline your offer of dessert. You will have the proper papers prepared for the sale I trust."

"Ah-yes. Of course. I'll have my solicitor deal with the bank and send you the proper documents for signing. Do so, return them and you shall have your money by Thursday next."

"I appreciate that, Mr. Wildethorne."

They finished the last few bites of their meal, rose from their table and after Scott had finished assisting Katie with her coat, he paid the bill and left the waiter a tip reflecting his lack of merit while Katie pinned on her hat. They moved toward the entrance in silence, each somber-faced and alone with their thoughts.

"Let me fetch you a cab, Katie. It's the least I can do."

"All right, just this once." Together, they left the restaurant and Scott hailed one of the waiting hansom cabs. After giving the driver seated above him Katie's address and his fare, he turned to assist her into the two-wheeled cab. Once she was safely seated inside and he closed the door with a decisive click, she turned to him, her face as lovely as he'd ever seen. "Thank you for a lovely afternoon, Mr. Wildethorne."

As the cab disappeared in the thickening afternoon mist, Scott leaned back against the nearest damp lamppost. He missed her already. He'd forgotten how the mere light musical sound of her Celtic lilt delighted his soul. *No more contact. Ever again.* He felt like the cracked sidewalk had opened up and swallowed him whole, sending him hurtling straight to hell.

Wayne Tripp

CHAPTER EIGHT

Wherein Miss McBride cuts through all the deceptive folderol and sets the record straight.

"So with Mr. Vanderbilt's bonus and the money from the two sloops we'll complete this week we should be able to hire the Valente Bros. to demolish the old warehouse and have enough left over to buy materials for three more sloops and our first airship. Brad over at Covell's Hardware Store said the train should bring the lumber first of the week. When Farnsworth's funds come, we'll be able to do more. I want to look into building catboats too. There seem to be an abundance of them around the bay, so I figure we'd be wise to jump on the bandwagon there and offer the public what's selling. That the way you see it, Josh?"

"Sure, Scott. Long as we give the sloops and catboats priority. I still think your dirigibles are a childish whimsy. Just so much hot air looking for a way to make us go bust. I don't think there's any future in anything that isn't on solid ground or riding the waves. But you're the boss."

There came a timid knock at the office door and a mountain of a man barged in, wringing his workman's hat between two ham-sized fists.

"Beggin' yer pardon, boss, but there's a lady here to see you. Showed up in O'Brien's hansom cab. Real treat for sore eyes she is, boss." Ulysses Truesdale was the Wildethorne shipyard's resident blacksmith. In fact, his yard moniker was Tin man, though the nickname had less to do with his steel-working skills and more to do with his obsession to impale every inch of his flesh with some sort of metallic adornment. Besides providing a much needed mountain of strength, Ulysses' herculean-sized body provided him with a huge canvas on which to display his collection of metallic gee-gaws and a full array of vivid salty tattoos. Yet, in spite of his prodigious size, Ulysses Grant Truesdale was uncomfortably shy around anyone wearing a skirt.

"I'm thinking' it's that same lady's been here before, boss, though it's hard to tell, her wearing goggles and all."

Scott put down his fountain pen and papers, his forehead already wrinkled with wonder. He hadn't seen or heard from Kathleen McBride in a good two weeks.

Wearing goggles was not unusual in the least, especially in the industrial Northeast with its collection of smoke-belching mills, cinder-spewing steam trains and dust-swirling motorists. Their boatyard was constantly awash with sawdust as well. Scott had three or four pairs of eyewear himself, each for a different purpose. But so far, he'd never seen Katie McBride sporting goggles; it'd taken him a while to get used to her pretty face hidden behind her fragile spectacles. Unless, it wasn't her at all.

"Goggles. Well, don't just stand there, Tin man. Show the lady in."

Scott put down his fountain pen and papers, his forehead already wrinkled with wonder. He hadn't seen Kathleen McBride in a good two weeks.

Wearing goggles was not unusual in the least, especially in the industrial Northeast with its endless collection of smoke-belching mills, cinder-spewing steam engines, and dust swirling motor car enthusiasts. Their shipyard was constantly awash with sawdust as well. When there was wind, which lately seemed to be every day, much of it was airborne, swirling around like mini whirlpools and blinding dust storms; a real devil to work in. Scott had three or four pairs of eyewear himself, each for a different purpose. But so far, he'd never seen Katie McBride sporting goggles; it'd taken him a while to get used to her pretty face hidden behind her fragile reading spectacles. Unless their guest wasn't her at all.

"Josh, if it's Miss McBride, maybe you'd better go too. Her aim might be off."

Before his yard foreman could make his escape, the lady in question stormed in. Goggles indeed. He waited a moment, expecting her to remove the darkly tinted eyewear. Surprisingly, she chose to keep the deep rose goggles on.

"Miss McBride . . . it is you, isn't it? How nice to see you again," ventured Josh, edging toward the door.

"Mr. Steele. Please forgive me; I need to speak with Scott . . . Mr. Wildethorne . . . alone."

"Good day then, Miss." Without another word, he turned and made good his escape.

As soon as the door closed behind Steele, Katie staggered and collapsed against the nearest table, apparently no longer able to keep her pain or fatigue disguised. Scott, who'd been watching with concern the whole time, was instantly by her side, carefully assisting her to the nearest chair, and gently easing her reticule and parasol from her gloved hand. Once she was seated, he gingerly lifted her tinted goggles away from her face. The damage he saw sparked instant fury.

Kathleen McBride's face bore the remnants of a cruel beating. From the purple-yellow ghost of a nasty shiner leaked a constant dribble of pained tears. Scott was surprised the savagery of the brute's fist hadn't broken her nose as well. Her left cheek was bruised and scraped, and her quivering lips revealed a freshly-healed split. Peeking out from the fancy lace trim of her high collar, Scott caught a glimpse of finger imprints angrily branded into the pale flesh of her throat.

"What manner of man does this to a woman? I'll kill the bastard!"

"I doubt anyone would ever credit Archibald Briggs with being much of a man. He's gone Scott—his new position has him loading cargo in New London. He left this morning. I came as quick as I could—to *explain* things."

"There's nothing to explain. He told me you and he are tying the marriage knot. Though for the life of me, Katie, I can't understand why you'd allow yourself to be bound to this . . . beast?"

"And you chose to believe him. You can be such a thick-headed fool, Scott Wildethorne! Those are *his* words, not mine." She allowed her body to collapse against his. Scott couldn't be sure if she was attempting to be seductive, or just feeling weak.

"If he's trying to win your affections, why would he do this to you?" Scott growled.

"He doesn't believe he needs to win my affection, Scott. Archibald Briggs believes he *owns* me."

"And you let him go on believing that. For God's sake, Katie, *why*?"

"Because, Scott, in a way, it's true."

"God, so my being there that day just made matters worse. God, Katie, I'm so sorry. I suppose he thought there was something going on between us."

"*Is* there," Katie dared, "*something* between us?"

Scott noticed she'd raised one slender, trembling hand between them, placing her thin glove flat on his broad chest as though preparing to shove him away. Seizing the hand, and pushing it behind her, he gently drew her into his embrace before responding, "Why Miss McBride, there's absolutely *nothing* between us."

"Please, Scott . . . don't toy with me. I believe you still bear me some small affection, and I can trust you. That's why I'm coming to you now. You must let me unburden my heart."

"Some affection," he said, releasing her with reluctance. "I freely confess to being quite fond of your . . . good regard." Moving to the other side of the small office so he wouldn't be tempted to press any unwelcome attentions on her sorely used body, Scott waited until Katie had reseated herself before asking if he might offer her some refreshment such as coffee, tea or sarsaparilla.

"Sarsaparilla, I think, would be most welcome . . . as long as it's chilled. I did enjoy the bubbly taste of it when I sipped some of yours in the restaurant."

Once he'd served her the carbonated beverage, and waited while she took her first tentative sip, he asked how he might serve her.

She giggled; her gloved fingers flying to her bruised lips and nose as the sarsaparilla's bubbles tickled her nostrils. "There's a switch, sir. I knew you were a unique man. Most men always seem to expect me, or any of us gentlewomen, to service them." She belched slightly, and clasped the side of her rigid corset as though in pain. As though suddenly aware of Scott's concerned look, she sheepishly confessed Archie hadn't confined his battering to her face.

"He didn't —you know?" Scott reluctantly asked, his anger already beginning to smolder anew.

"Sir, you're quite impertinent to even ask a lady such a thing, but, no —he's never done that. I've been able to keep his hands off me so far. Though, he can be rather insistent."

"Katie, let me give my own physician a call. I'm sure he can offer you something to alleviate your pain and my concern while allowing you to maintain the utmost of modesty."

"I can't see a doctor, Scott. If Archie ever found out, there'd be no end to the suffering he'd inflict. But Archibald Briggs is not why I'm here. There's something else we must discuss." She hesitated, demurely sipping her sarsaparilla before continuing, her face displaying concern as though faced with a thoroughly daunting task. "Scott, is there somewhere we can go more . . . private? I have a rather lot to explain and would rather not be interrupted."

"I still think you need to let me talk to the brute, and maybe bring along a few coppers I know. Seeing her shake her head, he sighed and said, "wait here and enjoy your refreshment. I think I know just the thing as long as you don't mind a little fresh air." He was out the door before she could answer.

In a quarter hour, he hustled her out the door, causing a few papers on his cluttered desk to flutter to the floor. Among them were a number of months torn off the previous year's calendar, each with dates circled in red and a precise scrawl of careful calculations. One bold sentence stood out among the neat figures: *I knew it!*

He carefully assisted Katie aboard *Rattlesnake*, saw to it she was snugly wrapped in thick coach blankets, and set sail. Before noon, they'd anchored the friendship sloop in a secluded deep water cove off the island of Jamestown's southern coast.

CHAPTER NINE

Our Hero deals with an old, familiar curse.

Scott stomped in through his office door and thumped his sodden derby atop a precariously-piled stack of papers and plans. He threw himself into his battered swivel chair and kicked both long legs to bang his muddy boots down on the desk. The paper pile slid to the edge and fell to the floor in an avalanche of giant white confetti.

"Dammit woman! What will it take for you to give me even a chance at forgiveness," he railed to the abused walls, already defaced with thumb tacks piercing work orders and plans. "I know I fucked up!" he roared, this time more at himself than the disinterested wooden boards around him. _I know. Believe me, I know. Even though she obviously adores that boy, every time she looks at him she must remember that night._ Scott swept aside the few papers brazen enough to still cling to his desktop, folded his arms across the battered oak to cradle his head, and gave in to the melancholy and regret that formed tears enough to spill down his cheeks.

A short time later, he sighed, irritated at his indulgent self-pity. _Did he really think taking her to dinner would make up for what he'd done to her? He could only start over, having reaped the_ *rewards of his own horrific mistakes.* Scott sat up, swiped at the moisture on his face, and loosened his cornflower blue cravat.

He looked around, not really certain what he was looking for. Something was nettling him. Something wasn't right. He stood, his fingers already working to undo the line of buttons to his new gray waistcoat. It was then, as the door behind him banged open and Josh burst in that he saw it. Bending to pick the evening copy of the *Newport Daily* off the scattered paperwork, he stared at the face looking back at him from the front page headlines.

"So you've seen her," Josh broke into his mesmerized trance. "Oh—why did I burst in—heard shouting in here, thought that she-devil might be lashing you with more than her tongue this time. Honestly, Scott, I don't know why you continue to . . . well, it's none of my business, I guess." As if seeing the storm clouds darkening Scott's face, Josh let his thoughts trail off. "Anyway, that's Helene Labrecque splattered all over the evening paper. I and some of the boys know her. *Knew* her. Danny took her out once or twice. Nice woman, worked as a typesetter for the Daily itself. Took one of them motorized growlers every day into work, rain or shine. All the way in from Fisher Street, down near Gull Lane."

Josh paused, obviously waiting for his boss to say something. When he didn't, Scott's best friend ventured forward. "The boys and I are taking up a collection. Money to help buy Helene a better plot in the cemetery. Something they'd normally never give a poor victim of murder."

"Count me in, Josh," Scott said with all the feeling of a zombie. "For whatever you come up short."

"Sure, Scott. Thanks. I-I'll leave you alone for a while." Fast as a flittering firefly, Josh was gone.

It was *her*. The blonde he'd seen in the restaurant. According to the paper, she'd already been murdered when he'd seen her. She'd been trying to say something to him in the Laughing Gull. Of course, he'd ignored her. Katie was there; talking to another, attractive woman wouldn't help his case. But she'd made a point of catching his eye, saying something silently across the way, even pointing frantically at Katie once.

He didn't know her, had nothing to do with her. *Not like the child.* Oh God, not again. *Why wouldn't they leave him alone?*

* * * *

As promised, Katie received the documents for the sale of the warehouse, signed them and returned them to the shipyard's solicitor. True to his word, Scott made sure she had her money by Thursday, delivered to the library by a hired courier as requested. Holding to his promise, he stayed away, and made no attempt at contact her.

Six weeks went by and Scott kept his promise. It killed him, but he made no attempt to see her at all. His sister, the brunette Katie had seen in the restaurant, who just happened to be there waiting for the weekly dinner date she had with her wayward brother, realized who the woman he had with him must be. Although she thought Katie a most delicately beautiful creature, she was disturbed to find her brother in such a bad way. They'd had a fight, Tess thinking it was past time her brother accepted the woman didn't love him, and moved on. To that end, she'd tried to fix him up with one or two of the eligible ladies she knew from Ten Mile Drive. None of them could drive Katie's ghost from his heart. Seeking his own cure, he threw himself into his work, pushing his crew to build more, superior Friendships and forming a special team to work on a secret project within the confines of the newly renovated warehouse.

The following week, another body was found. Once again, it was that of a young woman, most brutally used. Scott had seen her, the day they found her body in a wooded lot just off Farewell Street. Her face had been pressed up against the frost-rimed window of his tiny office, begging for help. Of course, when he jumped up from his desk, scattering a day's worth of paperwork and spilling a fresh bottle of India ink across half of it, she was gone. He'd torn open the door, and searched outside, circling the office and then wandering through the yard, but already knowing in his heart he wouldn't find her. She was one of them. He couldn't help them. They were already dead. *Why wouldn't they just leave him alone?*

CHAPTER TEN

A Crack in the Ice.

Katie was miserable.

Archie Briggs had been waiting for her the day she came home from sealing the deal with Scott. He hadn't done anything that day except stand dumb-founded as she marched by beneath his nose and unlocked her shabby apartment door. But several days later, after she'd deposited the money from Scott's bank in her meager secret account, he was back, waiting for her, blocking her doorway.

"I just want a few words," Archie began.

"Let me pass, Archie. I've got to put Nathan down," she said, indicating the sleeping lad cradled in her arms.

Archie had let her pass, let her get her young son into his cradle and tucked up. But when she returned, he was still hovering in her doorway, waiting. Waiting like a vampire, for permission to enter and wreak unholy havoc. She'd denied him, pleading a sick headache, and tried to shut the door in his face. At the last second, he'd grabbed her wrist and tugged her hand through the narrow space between door and jamb.

"You will see me. Now!" he hissed. "You owe me, woman!"

She'd pulled herself free, stealing back her hand as the door closed. Frustrated, he slammed the door, catching three of her fingers, badly bruising them.

Next to him, Scott shone like an angel.

Week after week, Scott was true to his word. He didn't trouble her with gifts or plague her with his presence. Oh God, why wouldn't he break the rules? She finally had to admit that she missed him.

She appreciated the fact that he respected her wishes enough to abide by them, but she missed him. He'd wormed his way back into her life, and although his presence threw a monkey spanner into everything, and he had no right to expect even a shred of forgiveness, she missed him. *Should she break her silence? Crack the ice, and perhaps see if they still had a chance?* More than likely, he'd moved on. He was far too good-looking to remain unattached for long. There was the brunette she'd glimpsed in the restaurant; no doubt he'd have them lined up outside his office by now.

Unconsciously, she clinched her fists in frustration, immediately shooting sharp pain through her injured right hand. Dammit! Damn *him*

* * * *

The day it happened dawned warm and sunny, one of those rare New England winter days when Nature seemed to decide to give its creatures a break and smile on them. Katie had just deposited Nathan with Mrs. Rosselli and began the long walk to the library. She hurried, and took her usual shortcut off Gull Lane, cut across Maidenhead, and was halfway down Fisher Street, where they'd found that poor woman's body, when she spied old Mr. Slocum speaking with two gentlemen and a lady in front of his dwelling. Katie knew Slocum slightly. He always waved or exchanged a friendly greeting. Once or twice, he'd stopped her as she wheeled Nathan by in his hand-me-down pram, and tried to start up a conversation. Already reeking of booze, he'd always tried looking down her dress.

Yet, Mr. Slocum was known to be the best sail maker in Newport, perhaps all of Rhode Island. People came from all over New England to have him custom make sails for their yachts, sloops or schooners. Rumor was, he'd once made an entire suit of sails for the New York packet in a week years past. Everyone wanted Thurston Slocum sails. You just had to get him working before eight and make sure he stopped before noon. Mr. Slocum habitually had a liquid lunch, and people said he drank so much you could hear it sloshing around like wine in a barrel during a bumpy ride.

Katie could only see one of the gentlemen, the other having his broad shouldered back to her, but the lady and her lack of interest was clear as glass. The man she saw appeared to be in his fifties, highly prosperous if his well-manicured moustache and elegant morning suit were any indication. The lady, also, was elegantly dressed. Much younger than the elderly gentleman, he obvious lavished much of his affection and money on maintaining his paramour or daughter. For her part, she affected the bored aire of the truly rich, utilizing her time instead to press herself on the second man; seeming to use every excuse to touch or tease him. Her lover, or husband, perhaps? Katie didn't really care, and moved on down the cracked sidewalk, her mind already considering the cataloging and shelving of a new arrival of books for the library.

As she moved down the way, she caught sight of a friend, Sadie Miller, going the other way, pushing her perambulator with her own little daughter cooing inside. Katie waved and continued on her way.

She'd gotten a dozen yards down the road when she heard a commotion break out behind her, and turned around to see what was going on. As she whirled around, two screams rang out, one coming from the wealthy lady with the two gentlemen, doing her best to tug the younger man away from the ruckus erupting from the nearest alley. The second was from the young mother, Sadie, as she caught sight of the first beast bursting from the alley. At last Katie caught sight of the pack of five half-starved strays, mangy mongrels setting up a ruckus of ear-splitting barking and snarling growls. Sadie appeared terrified. Her infant daughter added her wailing to her mother's screams as the dogs danced around the perambulator, barking and snapping at the young mother flailing at them with her furled umbrella.

Katie moved forward, terrified, but wanting to help. She stopped, noticing the neighborhood was watching; from windows and open doorways she saw them, watching, doing nothing.

 Of the sail maker and the wealthy trio she'd seen conversing on the sidewalk, the only movement was away, their only emotion, revulsion at what was playing out. They'd do nothing.

No, she was wrong. Even as the wealthy young woman put one beige gloved-hand to her lips and screamed again, the young man shook himself free of her grip, seized the gold-topped walking stick from the quaking older gent and charged straight for the pack of snarling curs.

The first three dogs fled quickly, driven off by harsh words and a few swipes of the cane; the fourth and fifth proved more stubborn, snarling, jaw-snapping devils. While the big black shepherd mix danced around, barking and lunging as though the whole thing was a game, the other, a scarred yellow cur, snarled and spit as it tugged on a corner of the baby's blanket, trying to tear it from the shrieking mother's hands. Two blows from behind, and it gave up the fight, chasing after its pack mates who'd disappeared back up the alley like fleeing ghosts. The man whirled around, and with a shock Katie saw that the young gentleman was Scott. With the borrowed cane at the ready, he took four long strides toward the remaining cur and stopped. He turned and stood corpse-still, stirring at nothing for a moment, almost as if someone had called out to him. The big shepherd seized the moment and lunged, snaring him by the forearm and shaking it as though he wanted to sever flesh from bone. Scott cried out, dropped the walking stick and followed it to the cobblestones. The heavy dog straddled his struggling body, unwilling to release the arm he now clearly hoped to tear off.

In an instant, Katie scooped up the cane and attacked the dog from above. Her first blow missed the beast entirely, nearly clipping Scott instead. The second connected; the jarring force of the blow knocking her back on her bustle. The dog ignored it. Two more, before he removed his slavering jaws from Scott's arm, and with a flick of snarling jaws, showered Katie with hot blood and slobber. By then, Scott was up on one arm, but as he tried to rise, the dog hit him again, driving him back to the cobblestones, slamming his head into the bloodied rocks. Katie screamed, a heady mix of frustration and fury, and drove the stick into the mutt's exposed hindquarters. It yelped, and turned to deal with a fresh victim. Without hesitation, Katie brought the heavy brass knob slamming down across the dog's slobbering muzzle with all the force she could muster. It yelped in surprised pain, and took off for the alley in reluctant defeat.

Katie dropped the cane, and ran to Scott's side. Halfway to his feet, his cornflower blue eyes widened in amazement. "You! Katie—what are you doing here?"

"I live here. What are *you* doing in my neighborhood?"

"Trying to talk Slocum into making a custom gasbag for my rich client's new airship. Course the coward appears to have skedaddled, so I guess the sale is off." He turned away for a second, and address the young mother who was busy cleaning the baby's blanket as she tucked it around her daughter, and tried to calm the squalling infant. "Are you all right, Miss? The dogs didn't bite either of you did they?"

"No, sir, they didn't—thanks to you. None of these," she said with a strong undertone of disgust, "neighbors of mine would help. It takes a total stranger to do that. I'm so grateful to you."

"It was nothing. I'm just glad you and your child are safe." He turned back to Katie, looking sheepish. "Well, I guess I'd better be going and see if I can return this," he said indicating the expensive walking stick, "to Lord Percival." He turned to leave, but Katie grabbed hold of his torn sleeve.

"Scott, you're bleeding."

He looked down, realizing for the first time she was right, his arm was bleeding from the dog bite, and actually quite heavily. Katie moved closer, seemingly oblivious to the blood flecks already spattering her skirt.

"Katie, what about your rules. Staying away," he almost moaned, his strength ebbing away as the battle fury drained out of him and his forearm began to throb.

"This is different. Come with me."

In a few minutes they stood in Katie's parlor. It appeared Nathan was already at Mrs. Rosselli's. The glowering landlady had met them at the bottom of the stairs, but Katie merely glared at her, held up Scott's arm and brazened her way past her to her apartment. Once inside, she'd led Scott through the parlor, past Nathan's crib and on into the tiny kitchen. He bit his tongue, trying to overlook the neatly made bed crammed in one corner near the crib, little more than a mattress really.

"Sit. There," she ordered, indicating one of three mismatched chairs in her shrunken kitchen. Tiny, poorly equipped; spotless. She crossed the room to a kitchen cabinet. He couldn't help but enjoy the sway of her hips, the swish of her small bustle as she moved away. Standing on tiptoes, he could see her battered high-buttoned boots and a small bit of tattered lace as she reached for a bottle on the highest shelf. Sliding open a drawer, she extracted a wash cloth and from another she brought forth a meager cache of basic medical supplies.

"You're lucky I sold you the warehouse. Before I got the money from the sale, these didn't exist. Roll up your sleeve." As Scott shoved up the torn sleeve to his suit jacket and rolled up the blood-stained shirt sleeve beneath, Katie dipped the wash cloth in water she drew off from a tea kettle and approached him. Gently taking his bloody forearm, she stroked down his torn skin, sluicing away blood and dirt. Once she was convinced the bare arm was clean, she turned to the brown bottle she'd brought with her, and sloshed a little of the liquid inside into the wash cloth. Taking his arm gently again, she prepared to dab his injuries with the disinfectant, seemingly unaware she'd positioned the arm so that his fingertips might brush against her breast. He did not. When she began padding the wound, he flinched and jerked his arm away.

"Oh, no, take a deep breath," she directed. If you think that hurts, you'll not like the stitching, which seems the only thing that will stop the blood flowing. Seizing the arm he tried to pull away with a stronger grip, she reached for a long, rounded needle. It looked like the kind a furniture upholsterer would use. She swiped it with disinfectant, including the thread that was already laced through the eye, and said, "Hold still. I'll be as quick and gentle as I can."

He held his breath, and studied her face, bent intently over his arm.

As if to distract him, she said, "You know, you were a real hero out there. I wouldn't have believed it if I hadn't seen it with my own eyes. Nothing like the old Scott I knew."

"I told you, I've changed."

"I guess you have." She clammed up, then, seeming to concentrate on tying off the thread, before carefully snipping the end with a pair of sewing shears. She then quickly swaddled it in a clean bandage. "There. Done. I'd still see a doctor."

She rose to turn away and replace her medical supplies, but he reached out, his fingers encircling her wrist, forcing her to remain, forcing her to raise her down-cast eyes, to look at him. "Thank you, Katie. Thank you so much. I don't deserve your kindness."

"You're welcome," she said, wriggling her arm free and scampering to the cabinet with her supplies. "I suppose you should leave and go find your rich client--before my landlady starts clucking to the neighbors."

"I miss you, Katie."

"What?" She whirled around, dropping everything from nerveless hands. "What did you say?"

"I miss you. I wish things could've gone differently—"

"I-I miss you too, Scott. I don't want to, but I do."

He was beside her in an instant. For a moment, he stood above her and gazed into her eyes. Her lips parted softly and she took a quick breath as tears streamed down her cheeks. "Perhaps we could—"

Words failed as their lips found each other.

"We shouldn't be doing this," they said, almost together as they each sucked in a deep breath.

Their kiss intensified, tongues flirting while lips indulged.

"Scott, we've got to stop," Katie said, breaking apart and shoving herself out of his arms. "We have no future together. It's been too long; too much has happened."

"I-I know. I should go." He grabbed her again, smothering her protest with his passionate lips. She didn't pull away at once, but let her lips linger, grazing his. He could feel the moment she gave herself over to her feelings. She relaxed against him and cupped her cheek in his hand, exploring her lips with his tongue.

"No—this has to stop," she managed to gasp, pulling back with difficulty as though she were a moth and he the flame.

"I'm sorry, Katie. I shouldn't have done that. I know how you feel. I had no right to take advantage of you or the situation."

"N-no," she agreed, looking away, then reaching down to pick up the discarded supplies. "No right. I-I think maybe you'd better go."

"Yes. Yes, of course you're right." He picked up his derby and the purloined walking stick and turned toward the door so she wouldn't see how crestfallen he was. At the door, he paused, and turned to face her. "One question, Katie. Why are you still here? With the warehouse money, I thought you'd be able to find better lodgings."

"It's for Nathaniel. Mrs. Rosselli watches him, and he seems to like her. If we moved, she might prove too far away." She said the last with her face turned away. Scott felt she might be lying. Her voice sounded like she was fighting back tears. *Did she really want him to leave?*

"Go, Scott," she sniffed. "Please, just go."

"I will, but I'll be dining at the Laughing Gull again on Thursday. My sister, the brunette lady you were glaring at the last time, won't be there. She's attending a suffragette's meeting in Providence. I'd be delighted if you could join me . . . as my guest. You know it's a very public place, and I promise to be a perfect gentleman. I-I won't attempt to kiss you," he vowed, and to prevent her from declining, she quickly added, "Shall we say around One?"

"No, I can't possibly. Well . . . perhaps. Good day, Scott."

As soon as Scott closed the door behind him, he felt as though a five thousand pound anchor had been lifted from his soul. He'd felt like a vessel "in irons", but after the last half hour, he felt there was hope. They were starting to move forward on a new tack, and with a fresh breeze at their backs, they might even have a future. His arm didn't even hurt. At least, he didn't even care if it did.

CHAPTER ELEVEN

***In which our heroine realizes she's beginning to fall down a
familiar rabbit hole.***

Finished locking up, Katie leaned back against her battered
door and let the tears come. *She was such a fool.* Perhaps it
would've helped if she'd stopped herself before she brought Scott
home like an injured stray dog. She shivered, remembering the
snapping, snarling pack of dogs and how Scott had waded into
Sadie's rescue without thought for his own safety. He'd been so
brave. *Katie, what are you doing?* She couldn't let him ruin her
life again. *You can't fall in love with him. Not again, you fool!*

Kathleen paced the short confines of her tiny flat.

A dinner date, in a very public, respectable establishment. And
he'd promised not to repeat his brazen behavior of the last hour.
No kissing. *But she'd enjoyed his kiss. Even she couldn't deny
that.*

She shouldn't go. It would break her own rules. She wouldn't
go.

She went.

They started seeing each other once a week. Taking it slow and
careful, they only met in public places, dining in respectable

waterfront restaurants, walking in the park, or riding horses down past Brenton Point or along the row of Nouveau Riche mansions. All very proper and platonic, except for an increasing frequency of goodnight kisses.

After one particularly passionate goodnight kiss, Katie reminded herself she was playing with fire as she hastened up the street to retrieve her son. Once again, he'd offered to wait outside while she relieved Mrs. Rosselli of her charge, and then drive mother and son home. She'd put him off with a flimsy excuse, but how long could she keep up the charade? If their growing relationship was one of those sloops he was so fond of, Scott seemed eager to crack on more sail, where she'd like to come into the wind, slow things to a pause, and maybe throw out the anchor. *Oh God, Scott drove her crazy!*

* * * *

"You like this Mr. Wildthornes, no?" Katie was thankful Mrs. Rosselli was behind her, giving the ties of her corset an extra final tug, and couldn't watch her face as she dropped her bomb. "You see enough of each other. I tink it must be getting serious."

She was right. Katie cursed herself again for being such a fool. She stepped into the elegant dress, shimmied it up past her stockings, over her underthings and onto her narrow shoulders. Mrs. Roselli's deft fingers began fastening the myriad of tiny cloth-covered buttons.

This had to stop. They *were* getting too serious. She had fallen over the cliff again.

"He's just someone I knew in Boston, a long time ago. An acquaintance . . . a good friend."

"A friend, ah. I am thinking you'll soon be sharing your . . . friendship between the sheets."

"Maria! It's nothing like that!" Katie jerked forward and away from her friend's gentle touch, whipping around to stare at her curly-headed neighbor. "He's a perfect gentleman. Kind, gentle . . . generous."

"And handsome. Let's not deny 'ow handsome you find him. Now come here and stand still so I can finish these buttons or you'll never be ready for your Prince Charming."

"He's not that. He could never be that!"

"Ah, No?" Maria finished the buttons, placed both of her worn hands on Katie's shoulders and turned her around so she could face her young neighbor. Katie felt herself begin to quiver, but was it from fear or anger. "And does this Mr. Never Prince Charming not like child? I heared he rescued Sadie and her child a few weeks back. Doesn't he like Nathan?"

"They've never met."

"Why not? Kathleen, you know I like you . . . love you like a younger sister, but sometimes you are so stupid!"

"He can't know, Maria. It wouldn't be right—I know how he'd react. What he'd insist on doing."

"You *know* what he'd do . . . dis man you *barely are acquainted with*. And that would be so bad? I swear I will never understand you Irish and your pride! You are a fool, Kathleen McBride! A fool in love."

"I know, Maria. God help me, I know!"

* * * *

She'd been worry-free; able to leave little Nathaniel in the capable hands of Maria Rosselli who'd already raised eight tikes of her own. She'd even realized the tense apprehension she'd felt having to deal with Scott again beginning to ebb away as the tide of heady wine flowed in. Then, on the drive back to her tenement, her Scottie had opened his gorgeous mouth and turned it all to ash.

When had she begun to call him _her_ Scottie? She mustn't do that! He'd asked again why she insisted on living in the slums when Coffin's manor at Devil's Leap was hers. He'd even volunteered to help her move in. At least with the money from the warehouse sale, she should've moved to a better neighborhood. Why was she still here?

Then, he went one frightening step further, and asked if he might meet her son, Nathaniel, when he escorted her home.

He had no right to ask that of her. And yet, as a man she was seeing on an ever-increasing basis, a man she knew had romantic feelings toward her, didn't he have every right? *Of course he did. Admit it, woman; if not Scott, who did?* And yet, how could she let him see Nathan, the product of unbridled, animal-driven lust? How could she reveal her deepest, darkest secret? And as for moving into Uncle Jebediah's house, how could she explain the very thought of setting foot in that horrid man's residence again made her skin crawl? A man who'd taunted her from their first meeting; freely insulting her and finding endless excuses to brush up against her, saying how it was impossible to soil a dove who'd already bathed in muck.

Scott meant well, freely expressing his opinion she should take advantage of the situation and seize what the old buzzard owed her. Heartbreaking as it might be, she'd have to break off her budding relationship with him. She couldn't bear the thought of watching him turn away when he learned the truth. Just as she couldn't bear her reoccurring nightmare of Uncle Jebediah's icy claws reaching from beyond the grave to seize her.

As she heard the knock on her door, picked up her reticule and parasol, she vowed to do it. She'd end their friendship that night.

* * * *

It ended in a terrible row.

Scott was too much of a gentleman to begin a noisy quarrel in the restaurant, but once they were both in his borrowed horseless coach and on their way back to her lodgings, he demanded to know what was going on. When she mumbled something about not having a future, he glared at her like she'd turned into a harpy.

"What do you mean, we have no future, Katie. I care for you—you must know that! Of course we have a future. If you'll just let it happen."

"No! No we don't, Scott! Too much has happened. I can never truly forgive you," she lied. "I keep seeing that night. Every time I look at my son, I see his father's face. I'm soiled, Scott. Broken. You deserve better."

"I don't want better." He tried to continue, but a glance her way seemed to assure him he'd run into a wall, and when a beer wagon pulled out in front of him, he clamped both hands on the steering wheel and clamped his mouth in a tight white line. Once they reached her house, he turned to plead his case, or maybe kiss her. Feeling herself grow weak in the knees and her resolve weaken, she opened the door, sobbed her good-bye. and bolted for her door.

CHAPTER TWELVE

It Gets Worse.

One busy week fled before the frenzied charge of a second. Days clicked by like whirring gears as they began a third week, and still they'd neither met nor spoke. Scott slammed down the receiver on the boatyard's aether-speak and stared out the frosty window at the slowly growing dirigible. No matter how many notes of concern, or open invitation to dine he sent by the whooshing brass tube of the postal service, they went unacknowledged. Likewise the half dozen aether-speak calls he made each day. *Damn it! What had he done?* Scott fumed at the fickle behavior of womankind, but continued trying to soothe his broken heart by with laying out his empire and letting the wench have her way. It was obvious beyond his financial assistance and platonic friendship, she'd never let anything grow. Romantically, she cared for him not a jot.

A day later, while still covered in grease from a steam launch's leaking hydraulic pump, he spied several disturbing articles in the *Daily News*. Another young woman's body had washed up on Easton's Beach, murdered in much the same manner as the last. A string of murders like these had occurred before, but the public had been spared these atrocities for many months. The coppers, unable to get a lead on the killer's identity, had hoped he'd moved on. Unfortunately, it appeared he was back. Also, there'd been a bunch of robberies, several of them quite violent, in the area of Gull Lane. Add to that a brutal stabbing of a drunken dollymop two streets over, and Scott barely took time to clean his oily hands before thundering out the door.

* * * *

Kathleen was seated in her rocking chair, humming an old Irish love song to herself as she fed young Nathaniel when insistent pounding battered at her door. She'd her restrictive corset loosened and shirtwaist undone so Nathan could suckle, her mind wandering as she envisioned another, larger head with the same unruly hair, bent to her breast. The banging on her door wrenched her out of her fantasy. *Who could this be? Who knew she was home instead of manning her post in the library?* In truth, it'd been four days since she'd set foot outside this door, she'd been so depressed.

She opened her door.

A desperate man on an all-important mission pushed in, shoving her aside none too gently.

"Damnit, woman! I was right to worry! You're such an innocent. You answer your door without first determining who's lurking outside. Katie, you're way too trusting. I could've been anyone—some undesirable rogue out to do you harm!"

"I see your point," she threw in his face. "You've illustrated it quite well, sir! Why won't you show me the honor of respectful courtesy and at least address me as Kathleen if not Miss McBride? We've been over this time and time again. I haven't liked being called *Katie* since I was a child of seven. And why are you even here?"

"To see *you*! You've answered none of my notes or calls, made no move to continue our . . . acquaintance."

"You got what you wanted! You have the land for your damned zeppelins. I would've thought you astute enough to realize I'd forgiven you as well or I'd never have parted with the warehouse. I assumed our last night together would 've made my wishes perfectly clear and put an end to it all. Pleasant as I admit it was, I assumed you'd moved on with your life . . . as I intend to move on with mine."

"But I thought . . . I'd rather *hoped* . . . ."

"We had a brief moment, Mr. Wildethorne. A long time ago. I was an infatuated young fool, and you were . . . *drunk*. Now, if you'll please excuse me, I have a son to care for." She held the door open, and backed against it for support. With her arms behind her, the thin satin of her dark blue blouse pulled tight across her bodice, emphasizing her bosom. Sensing his eyes drawn to it, she felt the color in her face begin to rise like flame.

For a moment, Katie thought he was going to touch her, bend his head with its unruly light brown hair to kiss her. *She wanted him to. God in heaven, wicked woman that she was, she wanted him to so very much.* But then he looked at her; the hurt look in his blue eyes rapidly hiding his desire. With the bravado of stout manhood, he said, "All right . . . if that's how you really feel, I'll go. Katheen, if I can ever help you . . . if there's anything I can ever do for you."

"*Do* for me? Go! Just damned *go!*" she pleaded, on the verge of losing control.

"Very well—I shall. I'll not disturb you again, Miss McBride. Please lock your damned door!" And he disappeared through that same door.

What're you doing, you crazy, silly woman? This isn't what you want! He's going, you idiot! He's waltzing out of your life again, and you're letting him go!

Without hesitation, she tugged open the door.

"Wait! Scott . . . *please*! Come back! We need to talk."

Hearing his name shrieked, Scott slowed and turned his head to see if he should duck.

"What is it, Miss McBride? Did you forget to tear out my throat for good measure?" Scott growled as he stumbled into a man easily his own size, though massively muscular and solid.

Katie cringed when the bulldog of a man shoved past Scott. An *angry* English bulldog.

"Archie! You're back!"

"That I am, lovie. And apparently none too soon. Who's this bleedin' swell?"

"Archie, he's no one you need be concerned about." Katie stopped and backed away from Scott, visibly shaken. "He was just leaving."

"Name's Scott Wildethorne. Now, if you'll just step aside, sir. I'll be on my way."

"Wildethorne? Ain't you the bloke got my Kathleen skewered up in Boston? Yeah, you're the toff what let that Italian bastard have his way with her . . . I can see it in your eyes. I ought to give you a good beating!"

"Archibald! Please! Mr. Wildethorne was just going. Please, don't pick a fight!"

In three steps, the Limey sailor grabbed Katie with harsh hands, the panorama of garish tattoos standing out on his rigid forearms as he exerted punishing pressure. He shoved her back toward the tenement. Scott could hear her sleeve tear from where he stood, and wondered how bad the bruise on her arm would be on the morrow. Now, he had *no* intention of leaving.

"Get inside, my little sparrow and see to Nathan. I can hear yer brat wailing from here. Me and this swell of yours are going to have us a little . . . understanding; providing your boyo here ain't afeared of facing up to a man who makes his living catching monsters from the briny deep."

"Codfish, by the smell of you," Scott volunteered, unable to keep the growing hostility out of his voice. "And none of it too fresh. When was the last time you took a bath, Archie?"

Archie's face virtually pulsed purple with rising anger. As if expecting him to take a swing at Scott any second, and spark their smoldering face-off into wholesale violence, Katie dared a comment, perhaps hoping to make Archie back down.

"Mr. Wildethorne is just back from the Pacific, Arch. He was telling me his adventures, hunting whales."

"That explains why I caught him standing here still chewing his blubber, doesn't it? Well, Mr. la-dee-dah Wildethorne, my Kathleen isn't a dockside Judy for you to poke at, so you best stick your harpoon elsewhere." Without waiting for a reply, he shoved Katie back through the doorway saying, "I told you to see to yer boy, woman. Go!"

Turning back to Scott quicker than a copperhead snake strikes, Archie poked one grimy finger in the middle of Scott's new waistcoat. "You, Mr.wilde and horny, git and never come back. You're not wanted here. You deserted my gal in Boston, and it sure as shite weren't you got her out of that house after her crazy uncle took a sick fancy to her. I was there then to help her, and I'm here now. I just got me a weekly run on a local coastal steamer. Be in port regular now, so me and Kathleen can get hammered together for life and give that little tike of hers a real dad. So, you just git and find yourself a willing doxie! This here lady is a real lady, and she's mine."

Scott seemed about to say something scalding, or perhaps use his fists instead of hot words, just as Katie came back into the doorway holding a small, well-shrouded child. With a pleading look in her tear-bright eyes, she begged him to leave quietly.

As if biting back flames, he left.

CHAPTER THIRTEEN

Our Heroine's Revelations.

"There, that should keep us secure until the tide changes and the sou'westerlies come up," Scott said as he worked his way aft and dropped into the sloop's cockpit beside Katie. "Plenty of time for our talk." He cast a concerned look at his passenger as though willing her to begin and half afraid he wouldn't like what she had to say. "Sorry today isn't warmer. You okay, Katie?"

"I'm still a little cold, Scott," she confessed.

"Here," he said, settling himself back against the edge of the cockpit and the hatch of the sloop's small cabin. "Snuggle into my arms—if you don't think it's being too forward of me—and we'll keep each other warm while you spin your tale."

"I can't think it's too presumptuous, can I?" she laughed in a husky voice. "I chose to come out here unchaperoned with you. I rather suspect, Mr. Wildethorne, I'm quite at your mercy."

"Do I make you . . . uncomfortable, Katie?"

"Don't be silly. I'm not some vaporous heroine from one of your penny dreadfuls. I'm here because I *want* to be, Scott." She wriggled deeper into his embrace, loosening her stiff corset and unbuttoning the top two buttons to her high-necked blouse as she got comfortable. "I hope you don't think *I'm* being too brazen, but my corset is pressing up against some rather troubling bruises. Besides, I'm feeling quite cozy and warm at the moment. Besides, it's *not* a tale I'm going to tell you. It's the bone-white truth."

"Okay, I'll be a good boy, and listen."

"Good. I do have a question for you before I begin. I pray you don't think me too presumptuous, but am I correct in interpreting your regard for me as a bit more than slight?"

For his answer, Scott took Katie's face gently in his hands, turned it toward him and kissed her tenderly on her bruised lips. Before she lost her nerve and focus, Katie forced herself to wiggle out of his warm arms.

"Well, sir, *that* is by far too forward of you! But, not totally unpleasant. I must admit." *This is how I got in trouble the first time*, she thought. "This is precisely the point I'm trying to make. I need to know that your attraction for me isn't just physical . . . that you care about me enough that I might reveal something truly upsetting. Something which might drive you away again, convinced I belong in the nearest asylum."

"Katie, you must know how I feel about you. You're the reason I came home from sea, to try and salvage something from the mess I'd left behind. Whatever it is, tell me. I'm not going anywhere."

Overcome with emotion, Katie wanted to throw herself into his arms, and sob her relief that he'd come back to her. For her. Aware of how vulnerable she'd make herself, she forced herself to sit upright, tidy her appearance, and launch straight into her explanations.

She chugged through her first words hesitantly, rapidly built up a full head of steam, and surged ahead until her story was virtually telling itself.

"Unable to deal with the disgusting revelation of my ravishment and pregnancy, my parents sought to distance themselves from the distasteful situation. I was at the mercy of my mother's eccentric brother, Jebediah, Several weeks after my banishment, hydrogen gas bursting from a touring dirigible over Harwichport made certain my parents would never have to gaze on their embarrassing daughter again.

Although Uncle Jebediah's house had none of the glamour of the imposing extravaganzas the nouveau rich czars of steam, steel, and rail were building along Newport's cliff walk, it was still quite impressive. His brooding manor squats on top of a rugged cliff promontory thrust brazenly into the wild North Atlantic. It appears to be constructed entirely out of granite, slate and ebony marble. Shortly after my arrival, the frightened housekeeper told me one of the walls contained a number of stones resurrected from abandoned New England graveyards. The old woman seemed little more than a hysterical corpse wearing widow's weeds and ragged petticoats. At first, I just scoffed at her."

Her Celtic heritage causing her to shiver as she wove her tale, Katie said her own random observations proved the truth of the rumor. She'd seen numerous stones bearing names and dated inscriptions belonging to the long deceased.

"We Irish all know removing anything from a graveyard brings wicked ill fortune. I should've had enough sense to flee the minute I saw the headstones buried in the east wall, but I was a desperate woman with nowhere else to go, and no one who cared a farthing."

"I cared."

"You'd showed it by fleeing away to sea."

Katie paused, and wriggled her bustled behind to a more comfortable position. She began again. "Perhaps you think my description of the Coffin manor straying from the point, but I only mentioned it to show how the house filled me with a sense of foreboding from the start, long before the pugilist-faced manservant opened the iron-bound door and led me straight to my disapproving uncle with his unwavering obsidian stare."

"Not at all. Explain however you feel most comfortable."

"Well, my first impression of my uncle was of a ramrod-rigid Yankee who had no remembrance of me, and obviously thought me a burden he wished elsewhere."

Lurching awkwardly against the rocking boat, Katie staggered upright, smoothed down her brailed-up skirt, and removed her wool coat. She began unbuttoning more of her blouse buttons. Scott looked uncomfortable, as though fearful she'd lose her balance and topple into the sea.

"Sorry. You must think me quite improper, but I've been feeling a bit over-warm ever since the breeze died." She clutched the neckline of her partly open blouse and fanned cool air downward between her breasts.

"It does feel a mite unseasonably warm. Wind'll come back up when the tide changes," Scott said, the look in his eyes making it clear he felt the heat too.

Katie quickly said, "Ah, let me see," when she saw where Scott's eyes were riveted.

"You were telling me about your uncle," he prompted, embarrassed he'd been caught.

"Oh . . . yes. I eventually learned that one of my uncle's many hobbies was entomology. In particular, he was an avid coleopterist. That's someone interested in beetles. They're just bugs to me, and I'd think to most other people, but my uncle was fascinated by them. You probably noticed the Seaman's library has an extensive collection of exotic beetles as well as the usual beautiful butterflies." A saucy wave, a bit friskier than its mates, rocked the sloop suddenly, sending Katie stumbling sideways, straight into Scott's arms. She forced herself up and retreated to the other side of the small cockpit, but not before she became fully aware of his arousal.

"You, sir, are an impertinent rogue. I'm trying to *explain* my situation to you. Anyway, that first day, my uncle looked at me as a most loathsome dun beetle, most unworthy of his collection." She brushed a wayward russet tress from her eyes; the breeze was beginning to pick up. The sky to the southwest was far darker than it had been a half hour ago. She shivered. She'd best get on with it. "He looked at me as though I deserved what had befallen me, and had begged to be impregnated."

"With Giuseppe Puccini's child?"

"Y-yes." She hoped he wouldn't notice she'd turned away, unable to look him in the eyes when she'd answered. "Will you *please* listen? I've a lot to tell you before we head back. Anyway, over time, my uncle gradually came to accept my presence, and for a while, I actually thought he and I might be growing a bit more than tolerant of each other. There were times he was almost civil."

"What about his servants? The fisticuffs man and the others?"

"There were three and of those only the Austrian house keeper ever tried to help me, and she found herself sacked for it. What I mistook for grudging acceptance from my uncle was actually the arousal of the old codger's perverted lust. On an ever increasing basis, Jeb tried to maneuver me into untenable positions so he could fawn and drool over me." She kept her eyes averted, suddenly embarrassed.

"And I'll tell you now before you ask, Scott. He never got beneath my petticoats, though it wasn't for lack of trying. To admit the truth, he made many a grab at my bodice before I could shove him away."

"Damn the man! How long were you forced to endure this?" Scott all but growled.

"Until shortly before Nathaniel was delivered. Luckily, Nathaniel wasn't an olive-skinned Italian my uncle declared he'd refuse to allow under his roof. Jebediah Coffin could be as narrow-mindedly prejudiced as any prosperous Yankee. Although Jeb never abused Nathaniel, I quickly became fair game again."

Scott made a sound of angry disgust, but Katie rushed forward, wanting to get the entire tale told. "To his lurid advances, he added physical assault when his efforts were thwarted. I spent many a night bruised and bleeding, huddled and shivering in fear and holding Nathaniel close beneath the blankets while I listened to my ranting uncle battering away at my locked door.

It was at this point that Archibald Briggs walked into my life. He'd been in the kitchen jawing with the one remaining maid after delivering ice for the ice box the night Jeb Coffin finally cornered me upstairs in the nursery with no escape. Archie heard my cries for help, and came running to the rescue. He pulled the old geezer off me, and promised if he ever hurt me again, he'd alert the coppers and the old buzzard would spend his last days in prison. Archie seemed to pop out of the woodwork uninvited several times a week after that. As grateful as I was for his protection, I never found myself romantically drawn to my self-appointed hero."

Scott rose, took a long look at the wind and waves and seemed to gauge their position by looking at the shoreline. When he turned to face her again, he was frowning.

"That why you allow him to believe he's your knight in shining armor?" he grumbled.

"He's not!" she assured him. *You are. Or you could be if you gave us half a chance.*

Seeing Scott seemed anxious to up anchor and sail out of the cove, she decided to cut her tale short and finish ashore. She told of the night Uncle Jebediah decided to have another go at her just as Archie walked into the nursery. She'd just finished feeding Nathaniel, and looked up to see her uncle leering at her. When she told him to leave, he lunged at her. Archie walked into the room just as the old man grabbed hold of her and began pawing at her clothes. He'd pulled her uncle off of her and shoved him out into the hall.

"So old man Coffin assaulted you in front of our son?"

"Yes, he…. Our son, Scott? *Our* son?" Katie felt her face redden, but made no move to deny it. "How long have you known?"

"Almost from the beginning. As soon as I realized the dates were wrong for Puccini to be the father. At almost five months Nathaniel's too old to be his. Once I realized that, I knew he was mine. Last week when I used the shipyard's aether-speak to talk with the Boston coppers who rescued you, they verified my suspicions. They all assured me they arrived on the scene *before* you suffered a fate worse than death. These were all policemen I'd trusted with my life. I believed them."

"He could be someone else's, Scott. Other men have courted me."

"I suspect they'd be queued up around the block, Katie, if you gave them half a smile. But I *know* you Kathleen McBride. You're a good woman, a proper lady. You were a virgin the night we made love. I was your first. I'm the father. What I don't understand is why you lied to me—why you insisted Nathaniel was someone else's. Why would you let them destroy your reputation instead of saying I was the father?"

"I was a teenager, Scott, and terrified. I'd almost been raped. And the man who I believed meant everything to me had just walked out of my life. Hell, you ran. So it seemed convenient at the time. Everybody already assumed I'd been ravished by the

Ruffian. My parents never would've accepted you as a suitor; a mere policeman and a Yankee to boot. We never could have married. But more importantly, I *know* you too, Scott. You've always been an honorable man. If you thought you'd fathered a child, you'd want to do the right thing, whether you felt something for the lady involved or not."

"So this is about your feelings?"

"It's about *your* feelings! How you really feel about *me*! I may be a silly romantic, but a woman likes to feel loved!"

She paused, hoping he'd sweep her into his arms, fearing he'd tell her to take her brat and go. He did neither. Instead he glared at her, or rather through her, deep worry turning his sparkling blue eyes to cold steel.

"Get in the cabin, Katie! Get in here now!"

Scott said it with such force she almost obeyed at once. Almost. "Where--in that little thing? Why?" she said, hiding her uncertainty by putting as much sauciness into her voice as she dared.

"Just get in this damned cabin, woman. There's a squall coming fast!"

She heard the warning crack of thunder seconds before wind-whipped rain pellets assaulted her. With a cry of alarm, she threw herself into the sloop's small cabin so fast she landed on Scott. Her clothes clung to her goose-bumped flesh and she began to shiver.

* * * *

They'd had only the one wild night together in Boston. Kathleen had been an infatuated romance-driven teenager with wild, raging hormones while Scott had been an enamored hot-blooded male too drunk to make wise choices. They had both regretted their rash actions, if not their mutual, growing affection.

By the time Scott turned around, already cranking the wind-up electric lamp for light, Katie was struggling to decide if she should fight or take flight.

"Scott, what's going on? What are you going to do?"

He smiled, and it lit up her world. She'd never seen him smile in Boston.

"Scott, if I hadn't had Nathan, would you still have feelings for me? Please—tell me the truth. I'm a big girl now. I can take it," she lied.

His reaction was immediate. He reached out and pulled her toward him. She flinched, surprise causing her to recoil slightly. He gentled immediately. "Katie," he said softly, "I have been in love with you since the moment I saw you. I just never felt I deserved you. Everything I did went wrong. Whenever I tried to help someone, they got hurt. Hell, I couldn't even help myself while I was wallowing in self-loathing and pity. Now I'm struggling to put my guilt behind me too, so I can start over and make something decent out of my life. Be someone you'd be proud to walk beside." Putting his hand behind her head, caressing her coppery hair, he drew her toward him. "I still don't deserve you, Kathleen, but God how I want you." His lips captured hers in a swift movement that felt almost desperate, as if to prevent her from having the chance to reject him again.

She hesitated at first, but then returned his kiss with obvious affection and passion. When he finally raised his head, she said, "Did you have to hunt monstrous whales to gain enough courage to face me and express your feelings? You do care for me, don't you, Scott? Or have I made a complete fool of myself again? I-I was afraid you'd be angry, or you would feel trapped by obligation."

"For god's sake, Katie, trapped? I was the one at fault. I seduced you, and then left you to deal with the consequences alone. I was a grown man, and you were barely more than a child."

"I was an adult, Scott, more aware of my choice than you were at the moment. And besides, you didn't know there were any lasting consequences. I should've told you right away, but I didn't want you to feel obligated."

Scott hesitated, wanting to get it right this time. Slow, gentle and easy, he wanted his every action to show how much he loved her.

Her blouse slipped down easily, but her soaked corset was a bit more difficult to maneuver. Standing, Katie turned to give him access to the ties. Once he had divested her of her upper body clothing, he began to jerk the buttons through the suddenly tiny holes in his shirt. His eyes never left her body. As he fumbled with his own clothes, Katie finished pulling her sodden petticoats off, and slid under the blankets on the bunk for warmth.

Scott cursed as he hopped on one foot, struggling to pull off his boot. Chuckling, Katie said, "here, let me help," and reached to grab his proffered foot and yank on his boot. The second one soon followed, and Scott all but jumped out of his pants and dove under the covers to join her.

Katie shuddered as he reached to pull her into his arms. His hands quickly began to explore the contours of her goose-bumped flesh until her breathing quickened and her skin felt warm and intensely sensitive. As he gently cupped her breast, he plunged his tongue into her mouth and began a courtship as old as time.

When they were both so heated they could barely catch their breath, he entered her. She cried out with surprise at the unfamiliar intrusion, but as he gently moved above her, shock was replaced with a burning need. His pulled away and bent his head until his tongue found one milk-slick nipple and began to flicker across it. Katie sucked in her breath and he began to move above her with quicker, almost desperate strokes. She sucked in her breath, again and again, and then the sound of her low moan was echoes by his as they found the release they sought.

"I love you, Katie," he said softly, rolling to his side and pulling her close once more.

"Scott—are you sure? This is what you really want? I couldn't stand it if we did this and you walked away again. Are you ready to make a commit—"

"How about I spend the rest of my life proving it to you?"

* * * *

The sleet storm ended a full ten minutes before their lovemaking. While Katie made herself "presentable", Scott pulled up the anchor and hoisted the sloop's big main and jibs. By the time he worked *Rattlesnake* out of the cove through a series of short tacks, Katie joined him in the cockpit, snuggled inside her warm coat again. The light touch of her fingers on his own as she handed him a steaming mug, and the twinkle of deep emotion dancing in her eyes warmed his heart more than any coffee.

"What is it? Why are you staring at me, sir?" she said, a quizzical look, causing one delicate eyebrow to arch. "Is my lip paint still smudged?"

"No, nothing like that, sweetheart." Scott felt color begin to creep up into his tanned cheeks. "It's just with the sun coming out, it's hitting your hair, turning it to burnished flame. Almost like a fiery halo. You look like a beautiful Angel, Katie. My savior."

"Oh stop it. You'll make me cry. I can already feel the heat rising in my cheeks."

But as Scott came about on a final tack, giving them a following sea and a swift run into Newport, he noticed Katie shivering in spite of her heavy coat.

"You still cold, Katie? My loving didn't warm you up?"

"It's not the cold. I was just thinking of my story. The part I haven't told you yet."

"So, my sweet Katie, shall we be talking about your uncle, or the enigmatic Mr. Briggs? We've got about a good thirty minute run before I drop the sails. Why don't you come aft with me for warmth, and finish your tale. That's it, snuggle yourself right against my chest while I man the tiller."

"I feel better already," she purred. "You're warmer than a steam radiator."

"I hope you're referring to more than my body heat. Time to talk, lady."

She told him they were almost done with her uncle. The lecherous old bastard had fallen down the stairs one night and broken his back. Jebediah Coffin's manservant found his lifeless body at the foot of the stairs the following morning.

"Seems like a damned good thing, considering how he treated you."

Katie nodded, as though almost ashamed to be seen agreeing; then went on to say how the worst thing was the doctor said her uncle had lain alive at the foot of the stairs for hours before he died. Worse yet, the look on his face far from being the relaxed slack look one expects on the dead, was one of intense anger as though Jebediah Coffin had died furious at the rickety old stairs that dared to trip him up. Katie hesitated, biting her bottom lip and looking to Scott as though there was more she wanted to say, but didn't dare.

"I'm ashamed to admit my first thoughts were in complete agreement with you. That and the deepest feeling of relief." She paused, taking a sip of her coffee, and gazing out at the sea before continuing. "The thing is, the doctor said he'd lain at the foot of the stairs for hours before he died. In excruciating pain, but still alive." She took another, deeper sip of the coffee, and looked across the cockpit at Scott, the glimmer of tears in her eyes. "I-I never wished that, Scott. He was an evil man, but no one, no thing, deserves to die in such agony." She put down the half-empty coffee cup and stared out at the tossing waves for a good long while. When she looked back, glistening tracks of tears stained both cheeks. "He died with a look of fury on his face, as though angry at the rickety stairs that dared to trip him up." Katie hesitated, biting her bottom lip, and staring at Scott as though there was more she needed to say, but didn't dare.

They flew by a worn-out, three-masted lumber schooner busy setting its hook and running out a healthy length of anchor line. Nearby, a brace of workaday schooners swung to their own anchors in the incoming tide while their idle crews subjected the newcomer to unwanted advice and horseplay. Keeping a weather eye on them and his own sloop, Scott waited for Kathleen to continue. When she'd been silent through three minor adjustments to the sails' trim, he suggested she explain her relationship with Archibald Briggs.

He immediately plowed into a stone breakwater there; Katie didn't want to talk about Archie.

"Well, you must know something. I know you said his amorous feelings for you are not returned, and he's not your hero . . ."

"I never met a hero, Scott. There were times in Boston, I thought you were my hero. But I was young and naive then. Now

I know there are no heroes, Scott, just brave men who do what needs to be done."

Up ahead, a steam tug snorted a final cloud of thick black smoke as it dug its shoulder into a Fall River liner's hull and shoved the white steamer toward the dock. Hovering barely out of the way, just waiting for the dock lines to be snugged home, all manner of steam and gear-driven bumboats waited their turn at charming the passengers' out of their coin.

Scott waited until he'd steered them safely past the steamer feeding-frenzy before pushing his query.

"Good thing we're only a couple minutes out from the dock. I don't like the look of that sky behind us. Looks like a cold front coming in. So while I try to get more speed out of this old girl, why don't you tell me about Mr. Briggs?"

"I met him the night he pulled my uncle off me. Look, he's a horrid man. Too quick with his fists. I meant it when I said I didn't want to talk about him. He's gone to sea again, and I'm thrilled he's gone. He terrifies me."

"Well, I'm done letting the likes of him hurt you. Here's the wharf coming up, anyway. Sit tight, I'll get the dock lines and drop the sails. Then I want to go see my son, and we'll get you packed. I'm getting you out of that hovel today, Katie."

They sailed on a few more minutes in silence, snuggled together, their love wrapped around them like a warm blanket. As Scott neared the dock, he punched a small brass button on the rear side of the cockpit. There was an immediate sound of whirring gears and something pneumatic building pressure. Deftly, he brought Rattlesnake into the wind, her sails fluttering like a flirtatious dancer's. Pressing the brass button again, two lines shot out from a recessed devise in the sloop's side, each line flying in a snaking arc toward steel-capped pilings. Katie heard a distinctive clank as the small, powerful magnets at the end of each line clung to the metal caps like sharks' remoras.

CHAPTER FOURTEEN

In which dastardly Archibald Briggs asserts his "rights".

Archie pushed aside the worn lace curtains again, and peered out at the flurries swirling down empty Gull Lane. *When the hell did it start snowing; and where the hell was she? Out gallivanting around town with you-know-who doing you-know-what, no doubt. Left her screeching brat with the neighbor again, too. Good. He'd put the fear of the Lord in the little bitch when she got back. She'd not be able to walk straight for a week!* Not since he'd been a slum lord in Whitechapel, and seen some of the ripper's handiwork close to, had he felt such a thrill of excitement. If he hadn't been short-changed downstairs, he knew he'd have one hell of a boner just now. No matter. He'd heard there was a doctor in Leipzig could fix him up just fine. All he needed was money. From what he'd learned, his Kathleen was entitled to plenty of that. Soon he'd have his hands on all of it. Now, what was that professor's name? Schutzenberg or something else foreign. He'd created a clockwork cock for disabled veterans like him. All tiny gears, springs and mini-steam pumps powering a big shiny brass prick. Just wait until this trollop married him. He'd have her body to play with as well as her inheritance. He'd assert his rights as man of the house real quick. He fully intended to pay the good Professor Schutzenberg a visit. He'd indulge himself, no matter the cost. Who cared what the Irish bitch thought once he had a ring on her finger and her under his thumb?

Just let him catch her with that dandy Wildethorne again. He'd teach them both such a lesson. As soon as his damned coastal scow had started grinding her bearings off Brenton Reef , it became evident they'd have to limp back into Newport for repairs. He'd roused two of the lads for help before they docked. Dirty Hands Bill and Long-faced Sam. Just let Mr. high-and-mighty Wildethorne show his face next to his Kathleen's. Archie would be happy to rearrange it for him.

CHAPTER FIFTEEN

And is now the wayward hero so well beyond fisticuffs.

Scott saw him first. He and Katie came around the corner, deep in conversation, and there he was, looking as belligerent as a shipyard pit-bull. Archibald Briggs, home from the sea with murder in his eyes.

Pulling the horseless steam-truck to the slushy curb of the cobblestone road, Katie shoved her brass-rimmed goggles back on the brim of her top hat before letting an apprehensive scowl distort her face. "What is *he* doing here?"

Shutting down the steam valve, Scott sat there a moment glowering and thinking. Coming round to the passenger's seat, he leaned in close to Katie and told her not to worry as he gently helped her out of the car. As she walked in front of him, clutching her furled parasol tightly to her bosom, he reached behind the truck's seat and retrieved his ironwood walking stick.

"Good day to you, Mr. Briggs. Sea not to your liking, or have you made a record-breaking passage we should all be celebrating?"

"A barrel of laughs, ain't you, Mr. Wildethorne? Just like a damned cheeky monkey. My old girl's got engine troubles. Bearings grinding themselves to hell, not that it's any of your damned business. I thought I told you to stay away from my

Kathleen. Oh—did you bring your dandified stick to give me a good thrashing for them old bruises? It's my business what I do to my wicked woman, Wildethorne, not yours."

"Archie, I've told you before—you don't own me!" Katie interrupted.

"Hold your tongue, woman. I'm having a civil conversation with Mr. Wildethorne here. Women—you got to beat them every once in a while, Wildethorne, don't you agree. Gotta show them their proper place. Otherwise, they get all uppity."

"That's enough, Briggs. Stand aside. I won't waste my breath telling you to apologize to the lady since every second word out of your mouth reeks of filth. But we're going inside so Miss McBride can pack. You can either stay out of our way or we'll find out which is harder, my walking stick or your skull!"

"My Kathleen's not going anywhere! We have a deal, and she's not going anywhere with the likes of you!" Archie let his toad stare slither off Scott and bore into the young woman beginning to wither beneath his sudden wide-mouthed grin. "You be forgetting our secret, aren't you, Kathleen, my darling? What's Mr. Wildethorne going to think when I tell him your deep dark secret?"

"Archie, you wouldn't!"

"You know I will! I wonder how long your fancy man will hang around once he finds out what you done."

"Please, Arch—*don't*. Just let me go. Please don't do this!"

Swift as a darting spider, Archie seized Katie's arm and yanked her behind him, shouting she should get her arse inside or stay and see her 'boyfriend' beaten to a pulp. She didn't budge. He told her to suit herself, and take a last look at her pretty boy's face because he and his friends were about to rearrange it.

As if on cue, two huge engine-room stokers stepped out of a side alley, ominously flanking Scott. Risking a sideward glance, he determined they'd each been picked for brawn, hopefully having little residing between their ears. With what he hoped was a reassuring look at Katie, as she pleaded with Archie not to do this, Scott altered his stance to reflect his past military and police training as well as experience gleamed weathering numerous bar fights.

"Well, Mr. Wildethorne, my friends Sam and Billy here are going to help me teach you some manners of our own. It's not nice to play with other gentlemen's . . . toys, see? Shall we begin the lesson?"

Billy led off the dance, lunging in from Scott's right clutching a broken barrel stave studded with three-inch spikes. Scott slipped deftly sideways, turning as he twisted, to face Sam, so Bill lurched past, tripping himself up on Scott's trailing ironwood stick. He went sprawling across the cobblestones.

"Oops." Scott volunteered, never taking his eyes off Sam.

Scott was half-right. Where Billy proved to be the cerebral-cretin he'd hoped, Sam was wily, obviously much better equipped with both physical and mental weaponry. Scott saw the raised pneumatic spike-driver seconds before he heard an enraged Billy staggering to his feet behind him. With a feint to the left, Scott dove toward the grease-smeared knees of Sammy's trousers just as he heard the loud whoosh of expelled air and felt the first spike dart by his ear. A guttural cry behind him told who'd taken the first nail.

Tugging on his cane's whale tooth topper, Scott freed his rapier from its lignum vitae sheath while Sam raised the pneumatic gun, aiming at his face. Scott's rapier split the air between Sammy's trouser legs milliseconds before the thug let fly with his second spike. The razor sharp blade dug into the thug's oil-stiffened pants, and sliced into his inner thigh, deflecting his aim. Scott cursed as the red hot spike tore a path of searing fire along the forearm he'd raised for protection.

"Damn, that hurts!"

"Scott, look out! He's got a gun!"

Behind him, Scott heard Katie's warning seconds before the first thug closed on him again. There came a resounding slap, followed by a woman's pained cry. Scott swore. He was going to *kill* this Archie fellow!

Whipping around so rapidly Bill actually took a step backward, Scott chased the thug into the nearest grimy brick alley, scaring Billy into firing his first slug prematurely. The shot went wide, burying itself in the wooden side of Scott's steam truck. By then, Scott had the huge cretin cornered in the back of the trash-strewn alley, and using the grimy brick wall, bounded up and over, his sword arm at the level of Billy's face, punching the thug in the side of the throat with the rapier's scrimshawed pommel. Bill dropped like a stone and lay still and quiet, alive but out of the fight.

When Scott raced back around the alley's corner, he was relieved to find Sam had fled. Yet his relief bled away in an instant as he turned to find Archibald Briggs with a razor to Katie's cheek.

"Mayhaps I was a mite premature in my thinking those idiots could improve your pretty face, Mr. Scott, but I sure as hell can rearrange Kathleen's. Watch me carve meself a sweet piece out of her cheek long before you can reach me."

"Let her go, Briggs. Don't hurt her. You've won. I'll back off and leave. There's no way I'm willing to endanger Katie. I can't stop you."

"But *I* can." Katie whispered in Archie's stuck-out ear as the triple barrels of her *Lady's Protector* Derringer grazed the soft flesh beneath his chin. "You're so predictable, Archie. Always staring at my bosom instead of wondering what I've got hidden under my skirt."

"You wouldn't dare!"

"Ah, but you know I would. Now, I've got three shots, but I'm betting the first one will be enough to splatter your puny little brain."

"Here, take her." The straight-edged razor was suddenly gone, as was Archie's bone-crushing grip. "She's yours, Wildthorne. Bitch and her screaming brat is more trouble than she's worth. Plenty other dollymops about that are far less trouble." Like the slum-weasel he was, Archie Briggs slithered by Scott and was halfway down the street before he dared turn and sling a final stone. "Oh—afore I forget, ask her about the secret we share. Ask her what I saw. Ask the conniving witch what she done, little Miss I'm-so-innocent."

* * * *

For a quarter hour they worked in silence packing Kathleen's meager possessions, awkwardly avoiding intimate contact, and dealing with the huge elephant hovering in the room. When Kathleen retrieved Nathaniel from Mrs. Rosselli, and Scott finally saw and held his son for the first time, the joyful emotion glimmering in his eyes matched the naked love glistening in Katie's. Yet, they said nothing. Only when they approached Scott's lodging, as she held Nathan modestly to her breast, did Scott sigh and shoot the huge mammoth squatting between them.

"You'll both stay here of course. I can sleep in my office at the shipyard. Won't be the first time. Luckily, Josh had me buy one of those new crank-up, electrik heaters. I should be warm as toast."

"Scott, you don't have to do this."

"I know. I want to."

"You could stay with us. I'm not exactly a pillar of modest morality."

"I'll be fine at the yard. Though, for the life of me, I can't understand why you haven't taken possession of your inheritance. Your uncle's house is quite impressive from what I've heard."

"I won't set foot in that hellhole again. That place terrifies me."

CHAPTER SIXTEEN

Wherein our heroine glimpses her own version of paradise.

It took less than ten minutes to unload Katie's belongings, settle in, and watch in frustration as Scott began to pack.

By the time he'd filled a worn-leather overnight bag, grabbed his coat and derby, Katie had removed her hat, brass driving goggles, and gloves. Sitting on Scott's threadbare sofa with its faded floral pattern, she removed her bolero-style suit jacket as she mustered her next question and looked up at her would-be savior.

"Why must you go, Scott? I feel positively beastly putting you out."

Looking up at him through her round-lensed spectacles, Katie's large blue eyes looked anything but innocent.

"I'll be fine. I'm sure both you and Nathan could use a little peace and rest."

Continuing to undress, Katie unsnapped the clasps to her corset, pulled the rigid satin and whalebone garment from her narrow ribs, and tossed it on a nearby chair.

"What if I said I don't want you to go? I'm still rather cold, Scottie. You could fix that."

"You're determined not to make this easy, aren't you? I'm *trying* to be a gentleman."

"It's not a gentleman I need just now."

Contrary to her complaint of cold, she continued to undress. When she leaned forward to begin unlacing her high-buttoned boots, she heard Scot mutter something under his breath.

"Scottie, please stay. I'll keep Nathan quiet and we'll stay out of sight so no one need know we're here. Please . . . we're almost a family already."

"I can't." The look in his eyes showed how very much he *wanted* to. "You're a good woman, Katie McBride. You've always been a lady to my mind. Once before I let the booze and my emotions get the better of my judgment, and it almost cost us everything. I won't besmirch and endanger your reputation further. Besides, I've been gone too long from the boatyard—if Josh doesn't watch the lads every second they'll have the bowsprits sticking out of the boats' sterns."

Although Scott seemed unable to drag his eyes from her tempting breasts or pouting lips, Katie's determined seduction back-fired. Seeming unwilling to allow himself to embrace her, or even kiss her good-bye, Scott stumbled out through the boarding-house door before turning and blushing his way through a hurried excuse.

"I've really got to go." He hesitated a moment, scowling as he stared at something behind her. "I'll talk to my landlady so there'll be no trouble about you staying in my stead. And I'll see you both first thing in the morning."

"You'd better. Now that you've met your son, I'm not letting you get away again."

But he did. By the time she pushed her tear-speckled glasses up her narrow nose, and began to rise off the worn ottoman, Scott had made his escape, quietly closing the door in her face.

* * * *

For Kathleen, the next five days were like living her romantic day-dreams. Nathaniel seemed drawn to Scott, who if not a natural-born father seemed dedicated to becoming one. As for herself, realizing she'd fallen deeply in love with the rogue, it was extremely comforting knowing his feelings so closely resembled her own. Though he seemed unable or unwilling to mouth the words, his every action clearly indicated how precious their moments together were to him. She began to believe, should the need ever arise again; he'd be there, standing beside her, protecting her.

They spent as much time together as possible, Scott sneaking away from the boatyard so they could dine, shop, or take a carriage ride by the mansions on Bellevue Avenue. For two nights he faithfully returned to his cold bed at the boatyard, but on the third, his modest chivalry collapsed, and they slipped beneath the narrow bed's cold covers together. They rose in the morning, happily exhausted and vowing between kisses to do it all again as soon as Nathaniel conked off for the night. After Scott left for work, Katie sat down at the battered table with a steaming cup of tea, eyes already brimming with tears. She was so happy.

Happy enough that when the newsboy dropped off the *Newport Daily News*, she never dreamed Archie's serpent had just slithered into her paradise. On the fifth night, after an evening of passionate lovemaking, Katie could stand it no longer. During the time they'd shared together in his lodging, she'd noticed Scott occasionally staring over her shoulder or off into space as if totally ignoring her words. It was so irritating! He'd just done it again, and when she'd questioned him about it, he'd brushed her off, mumbling something about it being a very old inn and some guests just didn't know when to leave.

"Scott Wildethorne, are you saying you want Nathan and me gone? I believe—you led me to believe . . . you *loved* us! Now you want us to leave?"

"No! Of course not! Why would you say that? You know how I feel about you, Katie."

"Do I?" Try as she may, she couldn't resist setting the hook in his skin. "If you don't mean us, then *whom* do you mean? We're the only people here, Scott. Look—you're doing it again!"

"All right, I'll tell you. It's about time you knew anyway. But after that, I want to know this 'secret' Briggs mentioned. I want to know why you're content to settle for lodgings here when you've got an unoccupied estate just waiting for you to move in. Your vile uncle's dead, Katie. He can't harm you ever again."

Reluctant at first to agree, Katie finally nodded acceptance of his terms, and Scott began his tale.

Surprisingly, he began with that fateful night in Boston. The night he'd been so roaring drunk he couldn't do his copper's duty and rush to Katie's rescue.

"Do you remember the father and daughter who plunging to their deaths from a dirigible?"

Katie shook her head affirmatively, but kept silent.

"Well, the daughter, that little girl haunted me for months afterward. Actually, physically appearing in my path and dogging my heels in relentless pursuit. I've only been able to banish her continuous harassment by drowning myself in the rum bottle. That was why I was drunk that night. I didn't mean to get drunk, but she just wouldn't go away."

Though her eyes had opened wider, Katie remained silent, so he continued.

"The last time I saw the girl, Theresa's ghost, was at the height of a violent storm in the middle of the Pacific. *Amazon* had a dead humpback alongside, men removing her slippery blubber as the water around them swirled with ravenous sharks drawn by the steady flow of spilled blood. When the sky to our west took on a yellowish-green hue and the undulating, oily surface of the sea began to boil, I was the mate on watch. I was forced to order the dead whale buoyed with a marker and cut loose. We struggled to hoist the cutting-in staging back aboard and secure it as the winds began to howl. With the whalers scrambling back aboard grumbling over the loss of precious barrels of oil, the violent storm struck. We lost two men in the first hour, while another three would nurse broken limbs for weeks.. Just abaft of the mainmast, I almost walked right into a shrouded figure huddled beneath a pile of dripping oilskins. Thinking it was some crewman too fearful to stand his watch, I pulled the pile of foul weather gear off the miserable figure only to discover two huge haunted eyes staring back at me. *At last*, the forlorn figure seemed to exhale. *At last you can deny me no more. You must know, Mr. Policeman, for I have followed you halfway round the world, unable to rest until I convince you I bear you no ill will for my death.* She paused for a heartbeat or two, as if remembering her terror as she plummeted to the ground. *My papa was out of his mind. Though we were cornered, I know you did not force us to jump. You must stop feeling guilty for what happened. My death was never your fault.* The lightning flashed once again, and she was gone, the night suddenly as black and empty as my heart. That was the night I first thought of going home."

"Have you, that is, have you seen her since then?"

He reached for her hands and drew her close. As she looked into his eyes, he said softly, "You do believe me, don't you, Katie?"

"As a matter of fact, I do."

"Thank God," he said, taking a deep breath. "I'm sure it seems a bit strange to you, but I continue to see the dead. I'd been seeing and denying their existence for a long time. They walked the deck of my whaleship and glided along the beaches of Maui. The streets and alehouses of Lahaina and Frisco were full of them. I saw the ghost of Lizzie Borden's murdered father haranguing her in front of the store in Fall River, and almost bumped into a man with a bullet hole between his shoulder blades staggering down the promenade deck aboard the *Priscilla*. And, they were here, walking the streets of Newport. Even in this very boarding house that had started life as a tavern run by a retired pirate. Here in the *Sea Dog Inn*, ghosts still walk. Sometimes, in these very rooms. I've seen them.

"Scott, *here*? In these rooms? With Nathaniel?" Katie's face blanched before she framed her next question. "While we made love? Mother of God!"

"I wouldn't worry too much on that one. She's a middle-aged woman, and was the old buccaneer's favorite doxie. She seems rather fond of our son. Always oohing and ahing like a jovial old grandmother. Don't worry about her, Katie. She means us no harm. Now, I seem to remember you promised to tell me a secret, my love. Talk."

"What if I pleaded fatigue, kind sir?" she cooed, winding her long fingers playfully through his chest hairs. "We *have* been cuddling for hours. A gentleman wouldn't dream of forcing a lady."

"I think we established several nights back I'm no gentleman."

"Then what if I begged your trust, and assured you," she hesitated for a single breath, as if about to hurl herself over a cliff, "there is no 'secret'. Archie made it up on the spot in hopes you'd abandon me and leave me to his 'tender mercies'. Thank God you didn't." She held her breath, knowing Scott's persistence might ruin everything she hoped for. Already nervous, she let her eyes dart about the room, afraid to glimpse whatever specter Scott claimed to see.

"Is she here? With us—now?"

"Who? Oh, you mean Molly? Our ghost? That's her name."

"You talk to her?"

"I-it's more of a mind-speak, but yes. She makes herself understood. But she's not here now. She respects our need for privacy. For a dockside doxie she's really quite a moral soul. Now, since I have no reason not to believe you, I think I shall. However, out of your own sweet lips I've heard you say how you'll never set foot in your uncle's house again, even though it'd provide you with lodging far more comfortable than these cramped rooms. It's not so very far from my shipyard you know; I could become your paying tenant if its fear of living alone keeps you from your inheritance. Of course, I'd set up in one of the distant rooms to maintain a proper decorum, but well within hailing distance."

"You would not! You're Nathaniel's father—I want you near him." Lowering her gaze, her cheeks flared red. "I-I want you near *me*."

"That could be arranged too. We'll drive out there tomorrow if you like."

"No! I'm not going there. Never again!"

"Why ever not? Your lecherous uncle is dead, sweetheart."

Doing all she could not to scream, Katie answered immediately. "Is he?"

"Well, now you know I can see the dead, don't you? As for his still being there, there's really only one way to find out, isn't there? Imagine what a waste it'd prove if you're avoiding your heritage in fear of the man if it turns out he really is just rotting in his grave."

"No, Scott. I'm not going back there! He is there!"

"Katie—don't you think it's time you told me what's really got you so spooked?"

Sighing deeply, she snuggled closer to Scott, surrendered her resistance, and began to tell him her truth.

CHAPTER SEVENTEEN

Wherein our plucky Miss McBride reveals something intimate.

"You already know I love books. When you found me, I was wearing spectacles and playing at being a librarian."

"I think you look very fetching in your specks." He touched her face affectionately, brushing a wayward flame-tinged tress away from her cheek. "Course, without them, I get a better look at your lovely face."

"I looked like a frumpy school marm."

"I had a serious crush on my teacher," Scott teased. "Until Tommy Atkins pointed out she had a heavier moustache than his dad."

"This is no laughing matter, Mr. Wildethorne!" Giggling, she pretended to scold him as a stern librarian would. "Are you going to let me bare my soul or not?"

"Far be it for me to prevent a lady from getting anything off her chest."

"Scott! I'm serious. Listen!"

Chastised, he looked so adorable what she really wanted to do was make love, but she composed herself and launched into her story again.

"When I moved in with my uncle I was delighted to find Blackbriars had an extensive library. Perched on the seaward side of the manor it commanded a beautiful view of the Atlantic, but I only had eyes for the vast rows of books. My uncle was quite a collector."

She used her hands as she became animated, clearly excited about the library. "The large room dominating one entire end of the house, resembled a true British library with rich cherry and walnut paneling, plenty of floor-to-ceiling windows protecting stained glass inserts, and numerous comfortable window seats offering a choice of sunlit cheeriness or shaded seclusion. There were the usual crammed curio cabinets, ornate suits of armor, plus three or four displays of exotic weaponry and artwork by various old masters and the new Impressionists. I remember a gaudy Gauguin, a Degas and two delightful Renoirs in particular. Judging by his collection of Hindu, Polynesian and African sculpture, it was obvious Uncle Jebediah had traveled all over the globe. He even had an extensive insect collection—oddly containing far more beetles than butterflies—and a number of moth-eaten wild beasts stuffed for display. But it was really the regimented rows of books that fascinated me. There were thousands of them, from very old tattered tomes with iron-bound hasps and dubious skin sheathing the covers to crisp modern penny dreadfuls and romances."

When she'd first moved in, her uncle was still quite active around the waterfront, and he kept but a few odd servants, so most days found her curled up on one of the sunny window seats, lost in a good book by Dickens, Bronte, or Jules Verne. Only with the help of the romantic adventures she found on the printed page was she able to begin forgetting the very real nightmare she'd endured in Boston. Then, after a month of gradual healing, a new threat emerged.

Uncle Jeb found fresh purpose in staying home. There'd been another young woman's body washed up on a nearby rocky beach. A nurse, still in the remains of her hospital uniform. She'd been brutally murdered, and Uncle Jeb said this one was just too close for comfort. He said he was concerned for my and the baby's safety. So from then on, my peaceful sanctuary of literary escape was invaded by his obnoxious cigar smoke and the sweaty man himself. Jebediah Coffin believed in pressing the flesh, especially if it belonged to some sweet young thing, be she stranger or close relative. Biting her bottom lip, Kathleen looked up at Scott, noting he seemed to be growing agitated, as though he wished he could reach into her uncle's grave and rip the man's head off. She shivered as she relived her nightmare, deciding not to reveal the disgusting details of what happened when the old man enlisted the aid of his man servant, Horace Gaunt.

As if seeing how distraught her revelation made her, Scott took her in his arms, cuddling her quivering body and smoothing away her hot tears.

"Enough, that's quite enough. I'm sorry I pressed you. But it's okay, sweetheart," he soothed. "He's gone. He can't hurt you now."

"But he can," she cried. "You've got to understand. Blackbriars could've been a beautiful home inside. I could be so happy . . . our . . . any family could turn it into a delightful, airy, sun-filled home." She wriggled in closer, Scott's arms closing tightly around her in a comforting embrace. "There are hundreds of cozy places to snuggle and wide safe corridors for children to explore. It's a place that craves the laughter of small children."

"Children?" Scott said, a delightfully, wicked sparkle in his eyes. "Then why for god's sake, why won't you go there? Why not seize your inheritance instead of shunning the place?"

"Because after dark it became a place of screams. Mine. My uncle's mind became increasingly unhinged. He began to lie in wait for me, giggling to himself; lurking in the shadows until I passed by and then leaping out at me with maniacal glee. His greatest joy seemed to come from reducing me to a state of shrieking terror. Sometimes his assault came out of complete darkness, launched at the top of a second floor staircase. I almost fell numerous times. I narrowly escaped broken bones, serious injury . . . or worse."

"The man was clearly a raving lunatic! Thank God it's over!"

"No!" Kathleen jerked upright. "No! That's just it, Scott. It's not!"

"But he's dead, Katie."

"Yes, and a big part of me is glad. I feel terrible about that, but I can't help it."

"It's quite understandable under the circumstances, I think."

"Just wait, and listen! This isn't easy for me." She forced a weak smile. "Please. Anyway, after the funeral and reading of the will dragged by, I found a day when I could gather enough courage to check out my inheritance and decide if I could adhere to my uncle's odd stipulations. I left Nathaniel with Mrs. Rosselli, rented a steam carriage and drove out to Blackbriars."

"At first, I found it delightful. Wandering alone through the maze of hallways and rooms, planning and day-dreaming of the sweeping changes I'd make. Imagine how much more pleasant it would have been if I'd known you were coming back into my life. You are, aren't you?" She hesitated, gave his hand a weak squeeze and flashed a nervous smile.

"Of course I am. For as long as you'll put up with me."

"You'd better. Anyway, I finally noticed the sun was getting low and thought I'd better start back. Mrs. Rosselli would be wondering where I was. With an armload of dresses and clothes for Nathaniel, I headed for my steam carriage. As I passed the library, I ducked inside on a whim, hoping to scoop up a novel I'd started reading before my uncle's. It wasn't on the window seat where I'd abandoned it, but after a little hunt I found it perched high on one of the shelves. I knew I hadn't put it there, but I put my treasures down, fetched a chair and started to reach for the book.

When I felt the back of my skirt being raised, I assumed I'd caught its flounce on the chair back and my upward stretching was lifting it. I really paid it no mind." Kathleen felt her face suddenly redden with emotion, and fought to keep the tears out of her voice. "But when I felt hands skitter over my waist and begin pulling at my clothes, I knew I wasn't alone. I fell. As I fell, I felt his bony hands on me, seeking my flesh. I screamed. Something tittered, and danced away. When I sat up, my gaze fell on my father's old pocket watch. It had been torn away from the ribbon at my hip during my struggle. It read five-fifty precisely, a time I knew all too well."

Kathleen stopped, and sat ramrod rigid, swiping at the hot tears pouring down her cheeks. Looking Scott straight in his sky blue eyes, she spewed out the point of her story. "It was him, Scott. My Uncle Jebediah. Or at least, his evil ghost. Afterward, I realized the room had grown cold just before I felt his hands on me, and there was even a lingering whiff of cigar smoke. My uncle always came into the library at five-fifty. I usually put Nathan down for a nap just before that, and he knew I often retreated to the library afterward. He'd wander in behind his wall of cigar smoke, intent on continuing his *games*. Always at five-fifty precisely. Like bloody clockwork."

"So that's the secret Briggs was bellowing about? The place is haunted."

"Y-yes," Katie whispered, with only a zephyr of hesitation. "Blackbriars is haunted by a monster."

"We could go there together, sweetheart." Scott drew her back into his embrace, his own eyes beginning to smart. "If he's really there, I might be able to see him. Learn why he won't leave you alone. Threaten him somehow."

"*If* he's really there? Haven't you been listening to me? You don't believe me, do you? You—the man who talks to ghosts no one else can see. Scott, I felt his hands on me!"

"Katie, I believe you! Let's confront him—find out what his spirit wants."

"I know what he wants! *Me*!"

"I'll be right beside you. I will protect you."

"No," she protested. "You can't. I'll never go back into that hellhole again!"

"That's a bit extreme, don't you think? We could recover more of your personal things and Nathan's. I could keep an eye out for your uncle and get you safely out of there."

"No! I can't go there! I'm sorry, but I can't!" Arms flailing and tears threatening, she stormed into the other room and slammed the door. After a few minutes, Scott rose, grabbed his coat and derby and slipped out into the night.

In the morning he was gone, with only a brief note of explanation. He said he'd been gone too long from his boatyard. Scott promised to meet Katie around nine and take her and Nathaniel out for a late breakfast. He told her not to worry.

Disappointedly, the three all important words she'd hoped to see just before his signature were missing.

CHAPTER EIGHTEEN

In which our heroine attempts to face her demon.

"You getting cold, Katie?" Genuine concern wrinkling his brow, Scott shot a worried look at the shivering young woman snuggled against him in the horseless steam truck. Near gale force winds off the North Atlantic shook the Wildethorne Shipyard truck as it chugged along the coast road, slowly winding its way toward Devil's Leap and Blackbriars manor. The winter morning dawned with the numbing bite of ice in the air. Though they'd begun their journey in the anemic warmth of noon, the icy draughts off the wind-swept shore quickly bled away the feeble heat, driving icy needles into any exposed flesh.

Katie shuddered again, wrapped both her black leather gloves around Scott's muscular arm, and laid her cheek against his shoulder.

"No . . . I'm all right. I-I just can't believe I let you convince me to do this. Even when the lawyer reaffirmed I have to spend an entire night in Blackbriars before I can inherit, you wouldn't let me back down."

She looked to Scott for some reassurance, but he kept his eyes straight ahead, intent on his driving. The wind had kicked up, buffeting the truck, and swirling snow flurries around like pale dust devils. "I'm sorry if you think I was unsupportive. You know you have to do this Katie. For Nathan if not for yourself. If after one night you still hate the place, at least you'll have an option to sell. As it stands now, you inherit nothing." He paused, dealing with the winding rutted road and a sudden violent buffeting off the Atlantic. At least Mr. Reynolds is allowing me to spend the night with you."

Neither of them mentioned the exchange Katie had witnessed between Scott and Mr. Reynolds when a thick wad of bills went into the lawyer's pocket.

"But this time, we're just looking around and picking up a few things. Right, Scott? We're *not* staying?"

"We'll be out in plenty of time."

She lifted her face toward his and froze until he let his gaze flicker her way. "You —you do think it'll be all right?"

"Your uncle, you mean? I'm not letting anything happen to you, Katie. We'll check the place out, get what you want to take with you, and leave. You *know* you have to do this."

"I know I should, but I don't *want* to."

Scott allowed a sympathetic grimace to color his face as he gave one of her slender gloved hands a reassuring squeeze. They really had no choice. Katie needed money. She had a considerable inheritance, but unless she stayed overnight in the place she couldn't claim it. Her only other option was to sell the place, and she'd already made up her mind she couldn't sell the place to some unsuspecting soul knowing there was a ghostly maniac stalking the halls. So Scott had convinced her to go with him to Blackbriars and do a little exploring. What he hadn't told her, what he had yet to convince her to do since she claimed her uncle appeared like clockwork in a certain time and place, was to wait with him at five-fifty in the library so he could see the truth of this specter for himself.

"We talked about this, sweetheart. There's really no other way. Ah—there's Devil's Leap. And *that* must be Blackbriars. My God—look at that!"

Scott indulged himself in a long whistle. "*This* is your inheritance, Katie? It's huge—sprawling. Whatever trade your uncle carried on during his globe-trotting years must've been quite lucrative. I'd doubt he'd even talk to a lowly blubber-butcher like me." Scott let the steam truck bump to a halt on the ballast-stone driveway. Most coastal town cobblestone roads began life as ballast in the belly of merchantmen crossing the stormy Atlantic, a cheap and seemingly endless source of rounded stones perfect for roadways.

Blackbriars wasn't as large or imposing as the Breakers, Marble House or many of the other mansions enriching Bellevue Avenue. Still, Blackbriars was far from the rambling *cottage* he'd envisioned.

As his steam truck wound around the circular drive and lurched to a hissing halt, Scott's gaze swept over the abandoned verdigris-shrouded statuary and thorny brambles of beach plums lurking in a forgotten garden. With its unkempt grounds, mismatched turrets, multiple widows' walks, and barred cages over most of the ground-floor windows, Scott could sympathize with Katie's reluctance to return to Blackbriars. The place reminded him of a haunted mansion straight out of a gothic novel. Whatever the interior appearance of Miss McBride's inheritance, its ominous exterior of gray and black was both threatening and unsettling. If this was the face Jebediah Coffin wanted his home to present to the world, one of ugly, brooding hostility, Scott could well imagine the old lecher might still be hunting its halls.

Scott didn't bother with a cheerful "we're here". He could tell by the way Katie tried fusing her body into his and tightening her grip on his arm, she already knew. Every fiber of his being roared for him to turn the truck around, and speed her out of there.

Instead, he got out, crossed to Katie's side of the truck and assisted her out onto the ballast-stone drive. Placing one leather-gloved hand under her trembling chin, Scott raised her face until she was looking up into his eyes. "This is it, sweetheart. If you can't do this, tell me now, and we'll just leave. Can you do this, Katie?"

Holding her chin aloft in defiant determination, Kathleen insisted she would do her duty. She buried her gloved hands in her fur muff as if to hide their trembling. "Mind your step as we approach the stairs, Scott. Stay on the path. Uncle Jebediah set bear-traps under some of the more isolated downstairs windows. He said they were because he heard an intruder prowling around outside, but I always had a sneaking suspicion they were to make sure I didn't slip out a window with Nathan and escape. Periodically, he would have them switched around; so I never could be certain which window had steel jaws waiting beneath it."

"My God, the man was a fiend!"

"He still is," Katie said as she turned away and pushed herself forward.

They walked up a shadowy walk to Blackbriars' mold-encrusted stone stairs. As they approached the heavy iron and oak front door, Scott noticed worn lettering chiseled into gray slabs embedded in the nearest wall. Tombstones—unclaimed, unwanted graveyard rubble sometimes bought for its cheap price—so the rumors were true. To save money, the old skin-flint had scoffed at the predictions of ill fortune bound to using gravestones and utilized a bunch of them in building his home. What kind of stern New Englander would build such a repulsive edifice?

"Scott!"

Katie's warning sliced through Scott's musings like a hungry barracuda through a school of fish. His attention focusing on her immediately. He followed the direction of her pointing finger just in time to catch a large man stepping around a snaggle of bull briar. With his squashed nose, few remaining teeth and the raspy croak of a damaged throat whenever he spoke, Scott felt certain the man had spent a few too many hours as a bare-knuckled pugilist.

As the big man lumbered toward Katie, one ham-sized fist still hidden behind his back, Scott instinctively raised his sword-cane to defend his lady. The ex-boxer's free hand shot forth with the lightning speed of a thrown punch, grasping Scott's cane with enough force to threaten snapping it, sword and all.

"I wouldn't, sir, if you value your toy. I mean the mistress no harm," the boxer lisped through his broken-toothed mouth. "I'm Horace Gaunt, the caretaker. I possess Blackbriars' keys, Miss. You won't be getting inside without these." So saying, his scarred hidden hand appeared with a stout brass ring loaded with a swarm of keys.

"Mr. Gaunt, I do remember you." Katie said. Scott could see by the look Katie flashed him as he lowered his walking stick none of her memories were pleasant.

"Still performing my duty, Miss. Hope I didn't frighten you too bad and there are no hard feelings."

Scott wasn't sure if the man was referring to his present actions or past transgressions for Katie had turned her face to glare at the caretaker, but if the pressure of her gloved hand squeezing his was any indicator, Katie must feel those past transgressions unforgiveable.

"Thank you, Mr. Gaunt," Katie said as she graciously accepted the clinking bunch of keys. "Mr. Wildethorne is here as my guest. I expect we'll be here for a considerable length of time, so you needn't wait for us to finish. We'll lock up."

"Yes, ma'am," Horace croaked. "Thank you, Miss McBride."

With a start, Scott realized he knew the broken-down boxer. His mind working like a team of well-greased gears, the final cog in his memory clicked into place and he realized he'd seen Horace "Crusher" Gaunt lumbering around the bare-fisted ring in Boston. In fact, now that the foggy-aether cleared from his mind, he recalled seeing the fight that ruined Mr. Gaunt; the day he'd taken a severe beating from dancing Knuckles Malone. Feeling he ought to deliver a knockout punch of his own to the caretaker's arrogance, and put him in his proper place, Scott mustered a no-nonsense tone and added, "Please be good enough to see that those animal traps outside the windows are sprung and removed. We don't want any accidents, do we, Mr. Gaunt?"

"No sir. There'll be no . . . accidents."

* * * *

"Mr. Gaunt seems to upset you, Katie. I sense disgust and not a little fear."

"I was never allowed outside unless accompanied by Gaunt, and then only as far as the gardens. Uncle Jebediah always wanted me within easy reach. Horace Gaunt was my jailer. He was always my uncle's favorite cur. Usually, I could escape my uncle's clumsy pawing. But not always. Sometimes, Horace caught me and held me for his master."

"My God! I should thrash the brute!"

"No Scott! It's all passed—I have you now. Let's just go inside and get on with this horrid business."

Five minutes spent penetrating Blackbriars' guts and Scott reached three disturbing conclusions. There were no visible ghosts. With Katie clinging to his arm, they'd stalked down several hallways and up a flight of stairs without seeing a single apparition. Of course, it was only mid-afternoon, but the sky outside had grown quite dark and threatening. Besides, the place didn't feel bad. No foul odor, no plunging temperature. In fact, as Katie had declared earlier, it was rather pleasant inside, as long as one didn't know its unsavory history.

The manor was like a giant mausoleum or museum housing the collected treasures and oddities of a wandering eccentric who'd spent a lifetime circumnavigating the globe. Priceless man-sized second dynasty vases stood side by side with full suits of Hapsburg armor heavily encrusted with golden Florentine ornamentation, all crammed beneath an endless art gallery featuring everything from such famous masters as Raphael, Goya, Homer and Beardsley to the dark, rumor-shrouded Pickman. Each door they opened revealed clustered treasure hoards, lurking in the shadow-filled light, smothered in dust, but obviously of considerable worth. Old man Coffin may have possessed a reputation as a particularly eccentric, hard-hearted skinflint, but his home revealed the lecher was perfectly willing to spend some of his accumulated wealth indulging himself in whatever priceless whimsy caught his fancy. Priceless artwork from the sixteenth century was shoved into spare rooms next to odd brass contraptions bristling with gears, pulleys, belts and miniature steam engines. Scott sensed here was a man used to possessing whatever he desired. Katie's persistent resistance to his advances must have driven him crazy. Scott could well believe the old lecher had been relentless in his pursuit of his virtuous niece.

The first thing prickling Scott like a black thorn from the brambles outside was Katie's obvious wealth. As her despised uncle's sole surviving heir, all of his collected clutter was hers to dispose of as she saw fit, as well as this monster of a house and the extensive grounds surrounding it. Scott's random glance outside as they passed one grime-smeared bow window revealed a sizeable well-protected cove just below Blackbriars' grounds. *There's enough room on the grounds surrounding that cove to build a sizeable shipyard. I'd love to know the depth of that cove. Looks big enough to shelter everything we could turn out in a season.* Already seeing the tantalizing possibilities of the cove as a sheltered harbor, Scott asked her if she knew who owned the rights to the beach and land surrounding the deepwater cove. When she blushed, and admitted she guessed her uncle had, he gained a little better idea of just how much Katie had inherited.

The second set of rodent-incisors gnawing their way out of his belly was Katie's tendency to find sunbeams in the darkest clouds. In spite of her declaration that Blackbriars might be turned into a fitting place to raise a happy, loving family, Scott saw it for the ugly monstrosity it really was. To turn this monument to a crazy man's perversions into a fitting home for their son would take superhuman effort and limitless funds. And in the end, Blackbriars would still be an ugly house. The cracked and mold-choked headstones imbedded in the black marble walls like some unwholesome rash said it all. This bramble-choked mausoleum would never be a good spot to raise anything but a heap of trouble.

The third thing was—suddenly Scott felt Katie's deathlike grip loosen, and with a quickened stride, she began to surge ahead.

"Katie, what is it? What's happening?"

"We're there. Nathaniel's nursery is here, and my bedroom is just across the hall." She stopped in front of an open doorway and smiled seductively before continuing. "I'd invite you in for a bounce on the bed if the circumstances were different. Instead, could you be a dear and go turn up the heat while I begin gathering our things? The controls are on the wall, just down there. It's freezing in here."

"Okay . . . but you're not afraid now? It's okay if I leave you?"

"Of course I'm still afraid, but you'll be right back. I'm really cold, Scott. Besides, we're at the rooms with Nathan and my clothing, and it's still a long way to five o'clock, isn't it. I'm afraid like a ninny I forgot to bring father's brass watch with me."

"It's only four-forty five. Plenty of time."

"Good. Just go, and hurry back."

Scott felt a twinge of guilt at what he planned. Starting to move down the hall, he shot another glance at his watch. It was actually five-twenty. Scott trotted down the hall, guilt dogging his heels like a pack of starving wolves.

Scott found the cluster of controls for the manor's huge heating system and woke the creature of steam. Almost immediately, he sensed a rumbling growl deep within the bowels of the bestial house. Turning around, his mind wrestling with the conflict yet to come, Scott almost missed the swirl of dark skirts as a woman emerged from a room between him and Katie's bedroom. He felt a sudden rush of frigid air slam into his face as the foul stench of the grave stung his nose. Knowing most other people would merely see some sort of glowing mist if anything at all, he wasn't surprised when the young woman, attired in an eighteenth century servant's uniform turned to face him, mouthed one word, and then scurried down the hallway in tears, dissolving as she fled.

Down the hall, a door banged open and Katie popped out into the hall, her small *Lady Protector* pistol already cradled in her hands.

"Scott, I heard a woman crying. Is someone else here?"

* * * *

Deep within Blackbriars' guts, Horace Gaunt finished stuffing coal into the maw of the manor's monstrous furnace. Following Jebediah Coffin's last directions he'd already tinkered with various dials on the ancient furnace, making damned sure the pressure relief valve was permanently jammed in the closed position. The stupid woman upstairs had made sure all this extra heat he was generating had somewhere to go, but when the captain gave the order, Horace would see that the valves on each and every radiator got slammed shut. Over time, with nowhere to go, unrelenting pressure would begin to build . . . .

* * * *

Scott thought about lying again, but decided if he wanted this to work . . . if he wanted *them* to work; this was not the time for secrets and falsehoods. If what he had planned bore fruit, their feelings for each other were already about to take a bad enough battering.

"Let's just say your uncle isn't the only one stalking these halls. Some sort of maid I'm guessing, probably she worked here while the British occupied Newport during the Revolutionary War." Scott saw no reason to upset Katie by telling her the apparition had spoken to him or what she'd said. *Run* indeed; not bloody likely with what he hoped to accomplish.

Kathleen's reaction was to tell Scott she was ready to leave. She'd grabbed two carpet bags and filled them with the few possessions most important to Nathaniel and herself. The tone of her voice made it crystal clear she never intended to set foot in Blackbriars again.

For his part, Scott glanced at his watch, held his breath and stepped off the edge of the cliff. "Before we leave, I'd like to see this library where you said your uncle manifests. Besides, I think I can get a better look at that cove from the windows there. It looks quite . . . promising."

"Promising?"

"For a shipyard. I saw an abandoned apple orchard to the east I could clear and turn into an airfield, should you decide to move in. I'm hoping to start building airships. Dirigibles."

"I know what they are. How can you be so . . . unfeeling? Scott, my parents died in an airship explosion. You're not building airships here! And I'm not moving in here—I thought I'd made that quite clear!"

"Y-yes. Yes you have. *Quite* clear. The library, Katie. Let me corner this uncle of yours."

Katie looked like she wanted to argue further, but seemed to swallow her angry objections, and demurely led the way to the library. Scott thought she probably realized if she wanted to build her case against moving into Blackbriars it'd help to hang around long enough to actually *see* her hostile uncle's phantom. Plus, she had to realize he wouldn't let anything nasty hurt her.

They arrived at the library after following a winding path leading past staring suits of armor, two damaged mummy cases and a small pack of stuffed predators. It was five fifty-one. As Scott reached out to grasp the brass gargoyle-faced door knob, he seized Katie's wrist with his other hand.

"If you want this to work , , , if you want me to get the ghost of your uncle to leave you alone, I think you need to come in here with me so we can be certain he'll manifest."

"No! I'm not going in there. You knew I had no intention of going in there! You lied to me, didn't you? Told me we had plenty of time to get out of here before *he* shows up. You tricked me, Scott—I bet it's almost five-fifty!"

"Katie, this is why we came here. So you could prove to me once and for all the ghost of your uncle stalks these halls and means you harm! Now's the moment to prove it." He opened the cherry wood door and stepped aside, expecting – well, *hoping* at least—Katie would see the light and obediently surrender to his encouragement. If as she claimed, her uncle's ghost appeared like clockwork, right on time, now would be the time for her to prove it. She had to be there, for bait.

As he waited, he gazed inside the library, half-expecting Katie's uncle to be materializing as he watched. What he did see intrigued him. The ornate suits of armor, Ming vases, and priceless artwork scattered throughout the manor's winding hallways were as worthless baubles compared to the treasure trove clustered within the library's mahogany-paneled walls. Just before him stood a collection of fascinating maritime developments, all brass gears, glass dials and miniature steam engines, their inventive purposes a matter of intriguing curiosity. Under different circumstances, Scott would've been fascinated. He saw a portable steam-powered engine that could be attached to the transom of a ship's launch, eliminating the need for rowing. Behind it was a powered winch that could be rigged to a ship's mast allowing a single crewman to furl all the sails at once. Next to that squatted a water-cooled Gatling gun ready to be mounted in an island trader's gig; ready to discourage over-eager cannibals.

Further in, a quintet of large glass domes stood against the library's far wall, each housing a prime specimen of the extinct Dodo bird. Quite extinct, and yet this gluttonous man had the stuffed corpses of five of them. Centered between them, another ponderous dome displayed what appeared to be a singular golden specimen of the fabled firebird. Here sat a greedy, unscrupulous man's supreme treasure trove. Dazzling. Disgusting and yet amazing.

Still, what vexed Scott the most was that Katie still refused to enter the room.

"Come on, Katie, don't be a child!" he said, unable to keep the irritation out of his voice. "You've come this far—Look, I'm here to protect you."

"How could you? You know my uncle means to hurt me, yet you insisted we come here. Why? Just to see what I'm worth—see if my precious cove could be of use to you? So you could determine if I'm heiress to enough wealth to fund your ridiculous dreams? I suppose you want to assure yourself I'll provide a constant flow of cigars, liquor, and . . . cheap women. Y-You're no better than Archibald Briggs! Do you even care about your son or me at all?"

"That's not fair, Katie! I don't smoke and you *know* I don't drink any more. As for other women . . . for God's sake, Katie, it's always been you!"

As if sensing she'd gone a bit too far, Katie clammed up and began to back away from the doorway. "Oh, let's just get out of here! We've got what we came for—Oh God, Scott, look out!"

The first poorly-aimed strike smashed Scott across the back of his head, whirling him around amidst a field of blinding, hurtful stars. He saw Horace Gaunt, covered in black dust, raising his coal shovel for another swing, and glimpsed Katie, conflicting portions of anger and fear warring across her face, as she cursed and fumbled for something in her reticule.

The second blow glanced off his skull, grazed his cheek, and drove him to his knees. Scott had an impression of Gaunt flashing a gap-toothed grin, a drizzle of spittle spraying from his lips. He heard Katie yell, "You bloody betraying bastard", but couldn't really decide if she meant Horace or him. Gaunt bellowed something back like "You murdering bitch!" just before two small caliber shots rang out. Scott felt the buzz of the first slug whiz by his head. He swayed, and fell to the floor, glimpsing a furious Katie glaring at him and the room beyond. As he passed out, he turned his head to follow her pointing hand and saw the rapidly coalescing phantom of her uncle Jebediah.

"Do you believe me *now*, Scott Wildethorne? You do see him, damn you?"

Almost the last thing Scott remembered was a sense of failing Katie again. Then the ghost of Jebediah Coffin flew at them in a fiery rage. Yet, the blaze of insanity in the specter's eyes was not the hungry need to feed his interrupted lust, but a scalding desire for murderous revenge.

CHAPTER NINETEEN

Hell hath no fury like a heroine scorned.

"How dare *you*!" Katie shot Scott a look she hoped would sear through flesh. He was scrunched against the passenger door, his bloodied head lolling against the blood smeared window. *How badly was he hurt? He better not die on her, the heartless bastard!*

"I would've given you everything, you cad! You took my body, my heart . . . I would've shared my fortune as well. You knew how much I dreaded that horrible place, but you insisted I go there . . . to face my uncle. You *knew* he'd try to kill me. Maybe, you *wanted* him to kill me! She scrubbed angrily at her eyes; scalding tears burning down her livid cheeks, making her feel weak. *I'm so damned foolish! You betrayed me!* "In time, I would've given you control of Blackbriars to do with as you saw fit. P-probably even let you build your damned airships! All I wanted—all I've ever wanted from you—was your love. You couldn't even manage that. Well, I'm never coming back here again! I'm done with this horrid place! And I'm done with *you*!""

Seeing his gaze wouldn't meet her face, Katie raised her voice in anger, determined to get his attention. Whether he was semi-conscious and coherent or not, she felt so shattered all she wanted to do was hurt him herself.

"Hey, Scott, I'm up here. Stop looking at my bosom. You get your truck after I drive back to *my* son. Then I never want to see you again!"

He looked at her then, his head lolling from side to side as though he was trying to focus. *My God, he looks really bad!* Seeing the pain and misery in his eyes, she shouted at the tiny pleading voice coming from her broken heart to shut up.

Katie felt blind with misery. Scott, her protector, had betrayed her. That brute, Horace Gaunt had tried to feed her to her dead uncle. And *he'd* tried to kill her.

Katie had no idea how she dodged her uncle's ghost long enough to get Scott back into the horseless truck. Maybe the near insane fury boiling in her blood leant her strength; God knew Scott was mostly out of it, lending her little help. *Did he ever? Men!*

He'd live, but he'd have one hell of a sore head for a number of days. And some pretty sore ribs. In her crazed fury, she'd kicked him twice with her pointed-toed boot. *He deserved it.* Horace Gaunt would live too. He'd fled at the first opportunity. The coward smacked his head on the door frame trying to dodge the two slugs she'd fired from her derringer. He needn't have bothered. She'd been aiming at the wall. After all, *she* wasn't a murderess.

When she found she'd wandered on to Ocean Drive, Katie realized she'd taken the long way back into Newport. She shot Scott another peek, a mixed-breed look, part concern and part flaming fury. He seemed marginally better; the cut on his cheek still oozing red, one hand rubbing the back of his head, the other clutching his ribs as though he expected his guts to tumble out. His glassy eyes had the look of a condemned man as he tops the last step to the waiting gallows. Still, he was awake and watching her.

She whizzed by Green Bridge, slowing as she approached the turn at Brenton Reef, the wild winter surf of the North Atlantic bursting against the worn rocky shore on the seaward side of the road. In the summer, this area would be alive with elegantly-attired ladies holding parasols and well-heeled gentlemen with their canes strolling along the shore, enjoying the salt air and sea breezes; the true purpose of their meandering walk, of course, was to see and be seen. But now it was a blustery winter day in mid-week and they pretty much had the narrow, winding coastal road to themselves and the hovering sea gulls.

Thank God daddy had been progressive enough to see that his oh-so-modern daughter learned to drive his machine before he banished her from the family and went off to die over Cape Cod. Otherwise, she'd still be stuck at that awful Blackbriars place.

Katie saw an isolated spot where she could stare out at the sea instead of looking at Scott. She pulled the truck over, and sat there looking out the windshield a good long while, letting the engine idle before she turned to stare at Scott and begin. Unnoticed, it'd begun to snow.

"I-I suppose you heard what Mr. Gaunt called me, and think you know my *big secret* now—you think you know what I must've done?" She momentarily lost her nerve, hanging her head and noticing for the first time that the left side of her pristine white blouse was quite spattered with Scott's blood. She certainly *looked* like what she'd been accused of being. A cold-hearted murderess.

"So now you know I'm a killer. Just like that woman a few years back in Fall River. Killed her father and stepmother. Lizzy Borden, I'm pretty sure that was her name. Me—I murdered my Uncle Jeb, shoving him down those stairs. God knows I had plenty of reason with all his hurtful words and deeds. Not to mention I had to know all of his vast accumulated wealth would one day be mine. *Of course* I'm the one who murdered Uncle Jeb."

She paused, swiping at the torrent of hot tears pouring down her cheeks, and glanced at Scott, hoping he'd come to her defense, deny her guilt. He just sat there rocking back and forth, holding and shaking his bloodied head. Saying nothing.

"At least that's what Archie convinced me any judge and jury would believe. Especially if he claimed he'd been an eye-witness to my vile crime. He decided to force his attentions on me instead. After a proper period of mourning—enough to still any wagging tongues— he expected to marry and move in with me as his new bride. You see, he's after my supposed wealth as well. He forced me to agree, threatening to go directly to the Newport constabulary if I didn't comply. After all, I'm a mere woman," she said, her voice riddled with bitterness. "Who'd believe me if he chose to accuse me? There, now you know my damned secret!"

She glanced at Scott who appeared on the verge of passing out again, but she chose to reveal the truth anyway as she threw the truck back in gear. "For what it's worth, I didn't kill my uncle, Scott. Archie did."

She glanced at Scott, a small, foolishly romantic part of her still hoping he'd take her in his arms. He was asleep. "Figures," she grumbled to herself as she took the first curve a little too fast. The snow was coming steadier, just determined flurries at the moment, but with the promise of a more serious storm coming. Like her tears. A promise of many more. She allowed herself a snarled "You bloody shit" before concentrating on getting back to her lodging as quickly as possible. *Time to end this damned disaster.*

* * * *

She retrieved Nathaniel from Mrs. Rosselli, saying next to nothing, and blaming her wet cheeks and red nose on the cold snow. Luckily, her infant son slept right through the short ride home.

Lurching to a stop in front of the Sea Dog Inn, she shot Scott a final glare while she gathered her courage. He was awake, staring sadly back at her. Flinging "Get outta here, Scott" in his face, she slid out of the truck, gathered up her slumbering child, and scurried toward her lodging without looking back, knowing her emotional downpour was about to break free.

* * * *

An hour later, eyes scoured raw and wobbly on her legs from drowning her misery in a whole bottle of cheap wine, Katie staggered past the front windows and noticed the snow had picked up. Scott's truck was still outside, the engine dead.

"Go home, you damned fool. I'll not forgive you this time, Scott. It's over."

Red eyes drained of tears and head pounding as if a thousand tiny monkeys were banging away with hammers, Katie lurched to the ice-blasted window forty minutes later. Scott's truck was still there, smothered beneath a growing shroud of icy snow. The thick, swirling snow gave every indication of becoming the winter's first major blizzard.

"Jesus, you damned fool idiot—go home," she scolded, instantly realizing she was in his home, and he had nothing but a cluttered draughty office to sleep in. "You made your own damned bed," she half muttered to herself, the first icy tendrils of worry skittering down her back. *What if he'd fallen asleep? He could be freezing out there. She wanted him gone. There was no hope they'd ever patch this up. She was furious. She hated him!* Sniveling in self-pity and loathing, she wiped at her nose and scrubbed the last of her persistent tears from her suddenly blanching cheeks. *Jesus, Mary and Joseph, she didn't want him dead.*

Quickly checking sleeping Nathaniel, she tugged her heavy winter coat over her wine-spattered nightgown. Stamping into her boots, she stumbled back to the window, now glazed with ice. Through the opaque glass she spied the dark hulk of his truck still parked near the side of the snow-covered road. *What if his injuries were worse than she thought? He might be bleeding or freezing to death.*

She stumbled down two flights of stairs and threw open the door, her rapidly sobering mind still wrestling with what she *would* do if Scott needed help.

Clinging to the railing to avoid slipping on ice, she slid down the front stairs, her heart in her throat as she forced herself forward. *What if he was . . . dead? Oh God, no!*

She skittered toward the truck, narrowly dodging by an abandoned snow-covered penny farthing. In the distance she thought she could hear the laboring engine of a steam-powered snow plow. Yet Gull Street itself was empty.

Scott's truck was gone.

CHAPTER TWENTY

In which our heroine drowns herself in an emotional tsunami.

Across the room another tea cup flew off the shelf and smashed against the floor. The full bottle of rum Scott had purchased eight months ago to test his abstinence shook in its hallowed spot on the bookcase, threatening to topple onto the worn carpet.

"Molly! Stop this!" Katie groaned, wondering for the fifth time when the headache powders she'd taken would begin to work.

"I don't have to be clairvoyant to know what you want. I can't do that! A lady doesn't go chasing after a gentleman she's rejected just because she's changed her mind! I must wait, and hope he realizes I was being a silly fool, speaking in the anger of the moment. So stop throwing this tantrum and breaking things! I already have one baby!"

Katie smoothed the golden hair back from her son's forehead and stared at the door, praying for a familiar knock. *Where was Scott? He had to know she hadn't meant it. She'd forgiven him days ago. Why hadn't he come back?* Her fiery fury had melted away with last week's grimy snow. Now, all she had was a broken heart, wallowing in guilt and self-pity. *Of course he hadn't pursued her simply in hopes of grabbing her land and money. He loved her. And his son. Didn't he? Of course he does—he's said it enough times, you dumb cow! Then where is he?*

As if to remind her she still had a man in her life, Nathaniel started making suckling sounds, kicking his chubby little legs and flailing his arms around to attract his mother's attention.

Katie looked lovingly at her son, dressed in the little blue sailor suit Scott had given them as soon as he found out he had a son. He was such an adorable child. So handsome. Like Scott, the father she'd thrown away.

"Just you wait a bit, your lordship," Katie snapped far sharper than she meant as she began unbuttoning the bodice to her shirtwaist. "You're always hungry." She could feel hot tears pricking at the back of her eyes, as she remembered the loving caress of Scott's gentle fingers on her breasts.

Finished feeding Nathan, she crossed the room to look out the window as she buttoned up her shirtwaist. *No one. He wasn't coming today. Again.* Moving aside her flowered hat, goggles and gloves, she loosened her constricting corset, flopped down on the threadbare ottoman and let the tears come. Yet after a few moments of waterworks, she dried her eyes, praying she hadn't smudged the makeup outlining her eyes too badly, and patted dry the tear-damp bodice of her best Sunday blouse.

Oh, all right. You win, Molly. I'm not much of a proper lady anyway. I'll do it. I'll throw myself on his mercy!

Lifting her chin with renewed determination, she set about gathering her things and preparing Nathan for travel. She could sit here like some weepy, sheep-brained heroine from a penny dreadful, or get off her bustle and go get her man back.

Feeling her fiery Irish nature beginning to beat a determined call for action, Katie bundled them both up and hurried out the door with Nathan cooing in her arms. She hoped it wouldn't take too long to hire a cab.

There were two, the coachmen sharing a late-morning bottle and a brace of ribald jokes. Using a saucy trick she'd employed once or twice before, Katie raised the flounce of her skirt above her high-buttoned boots as she hailed the nearest cabby. In less than five minutes, she and Nathan were bouncing along the sludge-slick cobblestones headed for Wildethorne's boatyard.

CHAPTER TWENTY-ONE

Foiled Again!

Hard at work inside the boatyard's tiny office, Joshua Steele finished the payroll, and searched through Scott's swelling maze of newspaper clippings dealing with steam and electric-powered airships for their growing army of bills. He planned on devoting the next hour to paying many of them. The postal tube had brought the welcome bank note from Col. Farnsworth an hour after they'd hustled Scott off to the doctor.

While his ship was laid up in Frisco for repairs, Scott had saved the lives of an elderly couple being viciously assaulted and robbed. Since then, the gentleman, Colonel J. W. Farnsworth, grateful owner of the Golden Coast Railroad, sent Scott a generous monetary gift every month—not only enough to keep their growing boatyard afloat, but to give substance to Scott's fantastic dream of building airships for Newport's Nouveau Riche. In Scott's absence, Josh was busy putting the welcome funds to good use paying some bills when he heard a knock at the door.

He barely had time to turn his head and see who was knocking before a young woman clutching her small child burst in through the doorway.

"Miss McBride—what the hell are *you* doing here? Get out!"

"Mr. Steele, please . . . is he here? I need to see Mr. Wildethorne."

"Pardon my saying so, but you've got some nerve, lady!"

"Please—I've come to make amends. *Eat crow* I believe is the local expression. Please, I need to see Scott!"

"Like I said, he's not here. We're lucky he's anywhere after what you did to him!"

"I had hoped he'd realized by now I didn't mean it."

"You didn't mean to bash his skull in? What *did* you mean to do? It took a dozen stitches to close up the cut in his scalp!"

"Oh my God! I-I didn't realize he was hurt that bad—you can't believe *I* did that!"

"What did you mean to do, lady? You split open his head . . . Doc says he's got a severe concussion. Had him blubbering and claiming he was seeing ghosts! Kept saying something about seeing your dead uncle. And some thug named Gaunt, an ex-boxer or something. He wasn't right in the head for days. First thing he did after the sawbones finished with him was to call your lawyer. Told the guy you and he had spent the entire night together in that mansion of yours. He lied for you—so you'd get your damned inheritance. He did that after he knew you had kicked him outta your life for good. Yeah, he sure wasn't right in the head. Besides, you fractured one of his ribs for good measure. Not to mention, you seem to have busted up his heart for good measure too. Get outta here, and stop wasting my time. Take your son and go!"

"I'm sorry, I'm so sorry. Please . . . I must see him and try to make this right!"

"Are you daft? He doesn't want to see you, lady. I'm thinking never again. Sides, me and the boys got him a room in a nice quiet boarding house and one of Madame Fong's girls is nursing him back to health." Sensing how distraught he'd made Miss McBride,

Josh couldn't resist twisting the knife he'd stuck into the woman who'd nearly killed his friend. "If I know Scott, he's got his mast sunk pretty deep in her keel by now. The last person he'll want to see is you. Now, *get outta here!*"

* * * *

Josh's final words triggered the squall of emotion Katie had been struggling to keep at bay. Her mind drowning in a typhoon of swirling passion, she fled back to the waiting cab. Halfway there, Nathaniel seemed to sense his mother's misery, quickly adding his own squawling to her tears.

CHAPTER TWENTY-TWO

Wherein Miss McBride becomes a damsel in dire distress.

When Archie heard the woman fumbling with her key and trying to soothe her bawling brat, he set his men in motion. The plan was simple, so simple even bonehead Pious Peter should find it easy to follow directions. On the left side of the doorway, Pete would seize the kid right out of her arms. While she was distracted, Mr. Rutter would seize the woman herself. For his part, Archibald Briggs expected to sit comfortably in an easy chair facing the door. Wildethorne's lone rum bottle was in his hand, now open and already half gone. He wore a huge predatory grin slapped across his face.

"There, there, go to sleep for me now, darlin'. Mummy hasn't given up yet." She seemed to be alternating between sniffing and trying to calm her child. "I'll find some way to get your daddy back. Ahhh!"

A man's hairy, heavily-tattooed arms shot out of the dark and plucked sleepy Nathaniel right out of her arms.

"My son! Give me back my son!" The woman turned and began struggling with the man who'd seized her screaming child. "Help me! Somebody help me!"

Seconds later, another man's hands grabbed Katie. One pale palm clamped over her mouth while the fingers of his other hand reeled her in, being none to careful where his fingers strayed, giggling the entire time.

"Belay that fumbling, Weasel. Give the bitch here."

Taking possession of his captive, Archie dragged her back to his easy chair, his dirty boot kicking over the mug with his remaining rum. Plopping back in the chair, he yanked Katie to her knees, his grin widening to a shark's.

"Well, my pretty Kathleen, you've led us a merry chase. Thankfully, wee Ralph recognized you when he dropped off the newspaper." He grabbed the near-empty rum bottle up in his hand, and smashed it against the side of the chair, spewing liquor and shards of glass all over himself and Katie. "Tell me love, what kind of drunk keeps a full bottle of rum gathering cobwebs and in plain sight? You did say Wildethorne was fond of his bottle."

"A man wise enough to realize what his drinking almost cost him. A man strong enough to resist ever losing himself in the bottle again."

Brandishing the broken bottle in his fist, Archie threatened Katie with the jagged glass. "I ought to carve you a new face with this, you slut! See if your fancy man wants you then!" Flinging the broken bottle against the wall, he turned on one of his henchmen. "Of course, I like your face just the way it is. It's your smart mouth I can't stand. Pete! Do shut up that bawling kid!"

"Blessed be the saints. Shall I make it permanent, boss?"

"No, we'll need the little tike to make his mum here more . . . agreeable, you moron. Take him in the other room." He waited until the big coal-hauler stalked into the small bedroom and slammed the door. "Now, my little whore . . . ."

"Archie, please—let us go! I've never given you any reason to believe I bear you the slightest affection. You must know I will never have any romantic feelings for you. Why won't you just leave us alone?"

Archie's savage slap knocked Katie off her knees, bouncing the side of her face against a worn ottoman. As Katie struggled upright, blood began to ooze from her cut lip and scraped cheek.

"You fucking slut! Giving yourself to Wildethorne behind my back! I should beat you to a pulp right now!" Katie's eyes widened as if fearful of his words. Archie lurched forward, throwing a phantom punch. Delighted when Katie flinched, he made no move to actually hit her. "Maybe I should give you to Mr. Rutter here—give your man something to piss his drawers over."

Katie shuddered; as if afraid the scrawny man with his scabby hands might begin touching her again. "Scott's gone, Archie." Katie began to tear up. "I-I told him to go away. I'll never see him again. He doesn't want me anymore."

"Finally, some good news! Well, I *do* want you and me bloody fortune and I'm going to make damned sure I get what I want! Weasel—bring this trollop! Fetch Pete and the brat."

CHAPTER TWENTY-THREE

Wherein Our Heroine is Spirited Away.

Within minutes they'd all piled into Archie's gasoline-powered machine. Katie found herself crushed in the back next to Mr. Rutter, while Pious Pete bellowed off-key hymns and drove poorly. Next to him, Archie bounced drooling Nathan on his knee. They maneuvered away from Newport's slushy waterfront quickly, Pete beginning to entreat the saints' favor when the howling wind added swirling snow flurries to the mix. Glancing out of the snow-streaked window, Katie tried to avoid thinking about what Weasel was beginning to do with his hands. She noticed a grove of gnarled, black oak trees, their twisted, bare-boned limbs flailing in the shrieking wind like a sea of lost souls begging mercy from Hell's deaf ears. *She knew where they were headed. Mother of God—No!* Slapping Weasel's probing fingers away, she leant forward to protest.

Archie ceased bouncing squealing Nathaniel, spun around with a sneer, and shoved a damp cloth across her nose and mouth. *Chloroform! Dear God—no!*

Giggling, Weasel ceased his incessant scab-picking and held Katie firmly until the drug took effect. In a moment, she fell back against the cold leather seat, no longer caring what was happening to her.

* * * *

"Now maybe we can get a moment's peace! Nathan, me lad, yer mummy's gone for a little lie-down, Why don't you do the same, like a good little chap?" He smoothed Nathaniel's fly-away hair and stared out at the angry gray Atlantic, hurling itself as it always had at the coast's rocky shore. "Me and yer mummy's going to have ourselves a good time in a little bit." Using one grease-smeared shirt sleeve, he wiped away the line of spittle that flecked his lips, and contemplated some of the things he intended to do to Katie once they were alone.

Pious Pete launched into another off-key rendition of "Onward Christian Soldiers" as they followed the winding coastal road toward Blackbriars, squatting like a forbidding toad, high on an isolated cliff.

CHAPTER TWENTY-FOUR

In which Mr. Gaunt learns how to please the captain.

As Horace Gaunt finished tinkering with the mansion's heating system he heard voices. Giving the jammed steam radiator a final whack with his huge wrench, he threw the tool aside and reached for the loaded shotgun he always kept close at hand. Slamming the bedroom door closed, he locked it and stomped down the stairs toward the voices.

Approaching the front vestibule with stealth, he slid the curtain away from the grimy window with the twin barrels of his twelve-gauge. There were three men, only one of them huge, but all oozing trouble. The only one he recognized was that arrogant fuck, Archibald Briggs. Carefully letting the door curtain slip back in place, Horace activated his fifteen-shot auto-load. With the push of a small brass button the weapon began to hum and the data-display on his Grossberg lit up. He smiled, watching the small woman being carried in the arms of the biggest thug. It was *her*. Miss high-and-mighty McBride. All the puzzle-pieces were beginning to fall into place. The captain would be so pleased.

Keeping his shotgun ready, Horace opened the door a mere foot and a half before firing a gruff challenge.

"What you want, Briggs? I'm not inclined to be letting strangers in when the captain isn't up and about."

"He's dead, you stone-brained coot, and you know it. You *know* me. These other gentlemen are my friends, Mr. Philips and Mr. Rutter. Besides, I've brought Miss McBride and her wailing brat with me. You gonna let us in? It's freezing out here."

"I *know* who she is! Surprised you brought her back here. I'm pretty damned certain she hates this place," Gaunt tossed out, his gravelly croaking voice sounding like a sick bull frog. "Her damned stuck-up boyfriend here with her? Fella used to be a copper up in Boston. He here too?" "No, Miss High and Mighty here finally come to her senses and chucked the cheeky bastard out. I'm her only fellah now. You gonna let us in or keep us out here jawing until we all freezes solid?"

"Why are *you* here?"

Archie began to snicker, leprous-looking Weasel joining in with a string of wet giggles. "Seemed only right to me this murderess be brought back to the scene of her crime and pay for her sin."

"Well, I won't argue with that." Lowering his shotgun, Gaunt opened the door wider and stood back from the opening so those outside could come in. "Bitch killed the captain, she *should* pay," he croaked. "Come in, come in. Get that door closed fast. I wanta keep the damned cold out."

CHAPTER TWENTY-FIVE

Wherein Scott realizes something is dreadfully wrong.

Scott groaned for the tenth time and told Madame Fong's girl he wasn't interested with the least offensive voice he could muster. He turned on his side so she'd get the message and stop trying to undo his breeches. *Must be getting better*, he thought, running his hand across the fresh band of bandages binding his ribs. *Doesn't feel like a damned deer's antler sticking through my ribs anymore. Should be able to get out of here tomorrow.* Scott knew the small Jamestown ferry, *Dumpling*, was coming into the yard the next day, and he wanted to be on hand to help out.

"What's that, Scottie?" Fanny was pointing toward his bare chest, where a two-inch hunk of ivory broke free of his chest hairs and dangled from a thin leather thong tied with a sailor's knot. "Is it a whale's tooth?"

"This? It's a tooth all right, Fanny, but it's not from any whaleman's prey. This bloody bugger wanted to make me her prey."

Scott could remember the shark's tale without closing his eyes. The day his whaleboat had been stove in and he'd lost most of his crew, they'd brought more back to Amazon than the dead whale.

He hadn't noticed it at first, but when they'd brought the whale's carcass alongside and he'd begun directing the rigging of the cutting in staging, he'd seen the big dorsal fin cruising slowly by the bleeding whale. Estimating the distance from the tip of the dorsal to the end of the lazily undulating tail he'd realized it was not only a man-killing tiger shark, but judging by the size, most likely the same shark they'd encountered in the water.

By then, the men assigned to begin stripping the dead whale of its blubber had seen the shark too, and refused to step onto the staging, outside the ship. Scott had considered ordering them to do their jobs, but his heart wasn't in it. This shark had scared him. Instead, he took a lance from the nearest whaleboat and when the shark made another pass, he killed it.

They'd hauled the big female aboard, and when they slit open her belly, they found her not only full of tiger shark pups, but out tumbled Diego's head. Although he would've found a ready market back in Lahaina for shark teeth, he'd only taken the one tooth, to remind him how close he'd come to feeding all of her others.

"What's wrong, Captain Scottie? You got a funny look on your face. Like you seen a ghost or something."

Something wasn't right. Although Fanny was clinging to him, doing her best to please him, Scott knew right away something had gone terribly wrong. Even though Fanny had stayed way beyond the time the boys had paid for, and was even now enthusiastically trying to raise his spirits, it didn't prevent him from sensing trouble. Disaster was standing right at the foot of his bed.

Most people believed spirits were tied to the spot where they died. Some, like Katie's Uncle Jeb, who'd met a sudden violent end, did seem to be bound to a particular location and only manifest at a certain time. Every day, they'd suddenly appear, just like clockwork. Yet, even that old bugger seemed to have summoned enough power to reanimate his specter in his favorite room in the mansion, his damned library.

Scott had found others, perhaps those who hadn't perished by such violence, seemed free to move about as they did in life. They could appear in the daytime as long as the light was subdued; and New England winters were full of cloudy days. Such appeared to be the case with the ghost from his former lodging, Molly, who stood at the foot of his bed, wringing her hands and looking greatly distressed.

Scott tossed Fanny on the blankets and rolled out of bed in one fluid motion. Halfway to the water closet, he glanced back to see an irritated Fanny painting on a fake pout as she rubbed one mishandled shoulder. By way of explaining his rough handling, he declared he had a sudden need to pee. It'd never do to try explaining how a much older whore had won his immediate attention.

Stalking into the bathroom, he made sure Molly drifted in behind him before he closed the door. Her appreciative stare as she gazed at his rigid manhood quickly dissolved to one of hollow-eyed worry.

What is it, Molly? Scott visualized in his mind. *What's wrong?*

Yer fine lady and yer darling little laddie— be in a heap of trouble, she wailed. Then the sad particulars poured out of her like a flood of tears.

* * * *

Scott rose out of the boatyard as fast as the no-longer-secret airship would fly. With winter setting in with a vengeance, work on the boats had ground to a halt, and Scott had employed much of his funds and most of his idle workers in creating the first of his powered airships. The contract had come from the Coast Guard to supply a patrol craft destined to search for marauding undersea raiders and smugglers. They'd ordered an airship that was not only fast and silent but well armed. A real blessing. Scott never dreamed its first engagement would be a personal rescue mission.

Disturbing details had spewed out of Molly as thick as a cloud of flies. She seemed eager to get out of her gut. Unable to accompany Scott herself, she'd repeatedly pledged to use the aether to send a message to those unfortunate souls still imprisoned at Blackbriars.

Scott wouldn't have to face Archie's thugs or the malingering Captain Coffin alone. A glance across the gondola at well-armed Ulysses Truesdale gave him some comfort. Knowing Josh was coming up by the coast road with a truck load of Newport coppers and some Navy friends gave him more hope. *Hang on Katie—the cavalry is coming!*

Pulling back on the stick, he pushed his ship into a climb, praying they'd arrive in time. Outside, the wind-driven snow seemed eager to stop them.

CHAPTER TWENTY-SIX

In which Archibald Briggs learns the secret of Blackbriars' library.

Archie thought it was plenty warm inside. Hot in fact, considering the time of year and the stormy weather outside.

Rasping to himself, Mr. Gaunt lurched back into the brooding mausoleum of a house without bothering to wait for the others to follow him. The cluster of thugs followed the caretaker for a good three minutes in grumbling silence. *What a god-damned maze!* The only sounds they heard came from the howling wind outside and a sense of guarded whispering surrounding them. Suddenly, Gaunt stopped and lumbered around, a jack-o-lantern grin still possessing a few yellowed gravestones nearly splitting his battered pugilist's face in two.

"If you really mean to punish Miss McBride, it has to be done in the library. If you'll just follow me, I'll show you. I think you'll be pleased with the captain's . . . arrangements."

"Whatever, Gaunt, you lead the way. One place is as good as another I guess. Jeez, you're really cranking up the old heat, aren't you?"

"Captain likes it warm, and he's the boss. Here we are, gentlemen. The library."

"Like Arch says, yer captain doesn't give a shit, you stupid bugger. He's *dead*, blessed be the saints! Ain't he, Arch?" huffed Pious Pete, dropping the moaning Miss McBride on the nearest brocade sofa in a graceless heap. "Damn, even a slip of a lady like her gets heavy after a bit."

"That's fine, Pete." Archie turned to the other kidnapper, barely waiting long enough to deposit sleeping Nathan in the nearest chair before giving his rodent-faced toady fresh orders. "Wease, give her a small whiff of this." Archie handed Weasel the balled up chloroform-soaked rag. "I'm not quite ready for her ladyship to wake up all bright-eyed and bushy tailed."

* * * *

Horace Gaunt moved to the other side of the library, striding directly toward the grouping of glass-entombed extinct birds. Pressing a small button hidden in the decorative brass base of the second Dodo, he stood back as the central avian display, housing the imprisoned faux firebird, swung aside to reveal a hidden door. Blocking the others' view, he rapidly punched buttons on the winking time lock, only standing back when the brass clockworks ceased whirring and the thick door clicked open. With one coal-smudged hand he gestured for the others to enter the concealed room, taking particular delight in knowing though Miss McBride had often languished away her idle hours in this library, she'd never suspected there was a secret room hidden behind the captain's "disgusting display of unfortunate birds" as she was so fond of complaining. She'd never had the opportunity to find out what lurked just the other side of the wall. Until now.

"It'd be better if you boys brought her in here," the gruff care-taker volunteered, holding the newly-revealed door open. "Captain keeps most of his personal *toys* in here."

As if curious as to exactly what the late Captain Coffin's toys were, Archie quickly disappeared through the door Gaunt held open, telling his friends to bring the woman and her brat inside.

Once they were all inside the hidden chamber, Horace Gaunt's hulking form blocked the open doorway. "Sure wish I could hang around and watch you boys see that Miss McBride gets the punishment she deserves for murdering her uncle. Unfortunately, I've got to see to one of Captain Coffin's final wishes." He started to turn away, paused, and then added with a slime-slick smirk, "There's a Kodak buried somewhere on that shelf over there. Captain likes to savor his memories. Feel free to take pictures of Miss McBride's demise. Do make it messy."

* * * *

Once Gaunt was gone, Archie turned to his friends, ordering Pete to take the slumbering Nathaniel back into the main library and keep him quiet. The big man protested, saying he knew nothing about taking care of somebody's tike. Archie insisted he do it, declaring he didn't care *how* he kept the brat quiet—it wasn't his kid after all.

Once he left, Weasel and Archie took a thorough look around the room. Obviously Jebediah Coffin's playroom was a torture chamber, but the diabolical captain had kicked his evilness to new depths, employing the latest of infernal mechanical devices.

"Hey Boss, what's with the four locomotives all headed in different directions?"

Archie looked where Weasel pointed and took in the four two-foot model locomotives, all dragging stained chains and headed in different directions like points on a compass.

"I see the steam engines and shackles, Boss, but what is it they'd be pulling?"

"I believe, my dear Weasel, we're looking at Captain Coffin's answer to the revered practice of drawing and quartering. The trains, of course, aren't really strong enough to do the job properly, but you'll notice the wheels are all like cogs, locking them to the track. Plus, I imagine that system of belts and gears connected to the steam engine over here does the real work. I'm guessing the toy locomotives were more for Captain Coffin's amusement. Of course, if you reposition the trains so they're two by two, headed in opposite directions, why then you've got a mechanized rack. The man was a genius. Mad as a hatter, but a true genius."

Looking at all the diabolical devices positioned around the room, Archie had a sudden epiphany. Of course! There'd been a rash of unsolved murders over the last few years, the bodies of gruesomely tortured young women sporadically washing up all along this coast. Archie realized he was standing in the murderer's lair. *My god! Jebediah Coffin was a murderer, just like the old ripper.*

"Hey boss—boss, look what I found."

Still musing over the revelation that Jeb Coffin had been the infamous local murderer, Archie took the stack of photos Weasel handed him without really realizing what they were. When he did look, he recognized several women's faces from the newspaper headlines he'd perused, only in these tattered pictures they were all screaming or lying with their slack faces in peaceful repose, quite dead. Proof positive that Coffin was the infamous murderer. Yet— what was this! One of the gruesome photos, less tattered than the rest, featured a young woman in a torn white nursing uniform. He'd seen her face but a few days back in the *Daily News*. And yet, Coffin had been dead for months! Swiftly thumbing through the rest of the photo pack, he found what he was looking for. Horace

Gaunt appeared in at least two of the cracked and stained photographs, restraining Coffin's struggling victims.

My God, this monstrous mansion is packed with murderers. Katie and her damned brat are the only ones who aren't killers.

Not bothered in the least by what he was, Archie took a good look around the room at Coffin's torture devices."Which one, which one? So many choices . . . so little time. Which one?" But before he could give it another thought, he saw something to set his black soul singing.

"Well, well—what have we here? Weasel, get over here and help me get Miss McBride tied up!"

"Boss, you feel that tremor just then? I swear I felt the whole room shudder. Look, it woke Miss McBride up. She's starting to come around!"

"Quick, help me get her on this! Grab those leather straps and bind her wrists!"

"Boss, you hear that hissing? There's more steam pouring into the radiators. Can you believe it, more damned heat! Radiators is clanking and quivering now. I swear your Mr. Gaunt has got the heat cranked all the way up. It's like a damned rain forest in here!"

"Good. We don't want Miss McBride catching her death now, do we? Quick, start unclasping her corset."

"W-what are you doing? Archie—stop that!" a barely conscious Katie mewled.

"Easy, my love," Archie scolded, placing a firm hand across Katie's mouth and forcing her back down. "We don't want you waking up too fast and getting one of your bad headaches, do we? Let the chloroform wear off, love. Sorry about Mr. Rutter's cold touch. He was an undertaker's assistant, you see."

Archie snickered at his little joke. Weasel Rutter had been an assistant undertaker at a New Haven funeral parlor, though his true undertaking was pleasuring himself at the expense of the recently-deceased. Unfortunately, he'd been caught, and narrowly escaped with his miserable hide.

"Weasel, get that skirt and shirtwaist off her. It's been me experience women are much more compliant with their clothes off. I want to get her trussed-up so I can use my persuasive powers on her."

"Thought you was going to threaten her with harming her kid, boss?"

"This'll be much more fun." With a big grin plastered on his face, Archie waved his hand around the room at all of Coffin's dusty toys. "Let's just say, I'm feeling *inspired*."

As soon as Mr. Rutter put his hands on her again and began fumbling with the column of buttons marching down her bosom, Katie began to protest and squirm.

"There, there, my love. No need to make such a scene," Archie sneered. "Don't let your delicate constitution throw you into a fit of foolish female hysterics. You know damned well what I want! Just agree, and avoid all this . . . unpleasantness. I'm dreadfully sorry it's come to this."

Archie began to poke through an assortment of medical implements clumped together on a filthy tray, whistling Molly Malone as he worked. Weasel giggled and backed away, content to drool over the woman and watch his boss play.

Katie struggled against her bonds, protesting in language totally unbecoming in a lady.

Archie Briggs seemed in no hurry to pick out his tool, holding several aloft so wide-eyed Katie could get a good look at the scalpel or syringe he clutched.

She began to scream.

"Now, now, my dear. There's really no need to make a fuss. You *know* what I want." Holding a particularly nasty looking blade before her eyes, Archie smiled and approached her front.

"I imagine this will be quite painful, my dear." As if about to prove his point, Archie let his razor-sharp blade hover a mere inch above Katie's snow-white breast.

Instantly, Katie's eyes grew even larger. She began to squirm.

"Ah, so now I finally have your attention. Actually, this looks as though it will hurt like the devil. Why don't you reconsider, and just give me what I want?"

"No! I'd never marry you!"

"No? We'll see about that! I'd prefer the whole package, but if you think yourself too precious for the likes of me, why don't you just sign over the deed to this dump and everything in it?" He grinned, and played the point of his blade under her eye, down her cheek and throat until it hovered over her bosom. He bent to cut her, the sharp edge of his blade not quite kissing her soft flesh. Yet, it was enough to make Katie cry out.

"Y-you bastard!" she hissed. I'll never give you anything! I won't sign over this house and I'll certainly never marry you!" she managed while she struggled against her bonds.

"Why ever not, my dear?"

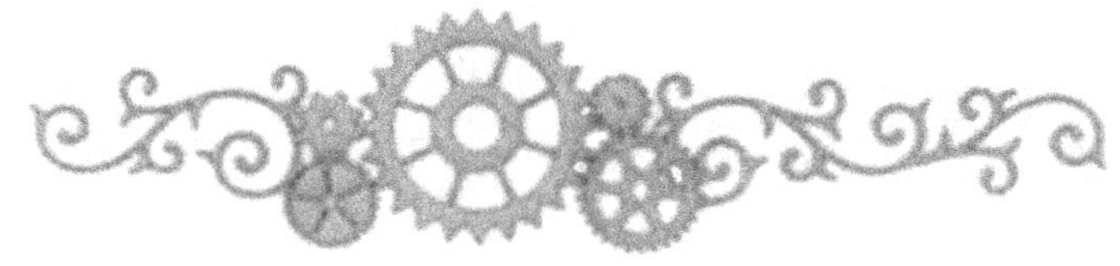

CHAPTER TWENTY-SEVEN

Our Hero to the Rescue.

"Because, she belongs to me, you parasite!'" an angry voice roared from the doorway. Scott charged into the room like an avenging angel.

Overlooked in the shadows, Weasel Rutter carefully jerked his scabrous body away from the wall. The clanking and hissing of the surrounding radiators masked his vermin-silent skittering.

"Scott!" Katie cried, squirming with renewed hope, her flailing fingers struggling to break free of her bonds. "Oh Scottie," she cried. "You came after me!"

For an answer, Scott stalked into the room, whisking his blade from its cane scabbard as he moved, keeping Archie at bay as he quickly severed the knotted rope binding Katie's left wrist.

"I seem to be having trouble staying away from you, woman," he laughed, his razor-edged blade freeing her right wrist as well. "Besides, don't you remember me claiming the honor of your hand?" he asked'

Struggling to rise from the wooden device she'd been bound to, Katie flopped back, suddenly feeling quite woozy. Her raw wrists were screaming in agony, and her rubbery knees just wouldn't work. "I don't remember being *asked*, Mr. Wildethorne," she scolded, glaring at Archie Briggs as he sat fuming in his chair, his every move challenged by Scott's thirsty sword point. Turning away for a pinch of privacy, she closed her ruined blouse as best she could with half its buttons missing. Then, steadied by purpose, she strode across the room and slapped Archibald Briggs across the face as hard as she could. As Archie's head rocked backward with a bloodied maw, she called him the vilest Celtic word she remembered from her father's cursing, and spit in his face for good measure.

Slithering unnoticed from across the room, Weasel's filth-encrusted blade rose like a hunting viper to center on Scott's back.

About to strike, he suddenly felt the insistent pressure of a police *Eliminator's* barrel pressed into the scabby side of his skull.

"Not so fast there, Squirt. Drop the knife," bellowed a giant of a man, rattling with bits of glittering metal.

While Scott was distracted, Archie rose from his chair, shoved Katie aside and made a dash for the door, screaming for Pious Pete to bash the brat's brains in.

Stumbling to her feet, Katie gave chase, shrieking for Archie to spare her child. He batted her aside again like a bothersome insect.

* * * *

As Scott darted after her, Katie stumbled across his path, sending him sprawling and his sword clattering across the planked floor. Rising from the floor, Scott noticed the time on his Navigator chronometer. It was five forty-six.

When he asked Katie if she was all right, she told him to ignore her and go after Archie—he was going to murder their son. Reluctant to leave her, he rose and moved toward the chamber door, finding a fuming Briggs arguing with his huge henchman. It seemed Pious Pete had serious qualms about snuffing out the life of a child.

As he hurried away, Scott glimpsed Katie already sitting up, moving to preserve her modesty and hook up her boots. Glimpsing her face, he saw fierce determination. Whatever horrors she'd endured, Katie was far from defeated.

Holding his sword to the side, Scott closed in on Archie Briggs in four quick strides. At the last second, Pious Pete lumbered directly in his path, still holding his son. Scott had to dance aside in order to avoid skewering his first born. The motion carried him through the doorway and out into the main library. When he turned, about to go back, Pete lurched toward him, holding forth the now wailing Nathaniel and pleading, "You take him."

Placing Nathan safely on the rug between two cushions, Scott watched as the giant lumbered out of the library. Then he turned to rush back into the secret chamber. As he did, the heavy door slammed shut in his face. Trapped inside, Katie was alone with Archibald Briggs. Scott's chronometer read precisely five-forty eight.

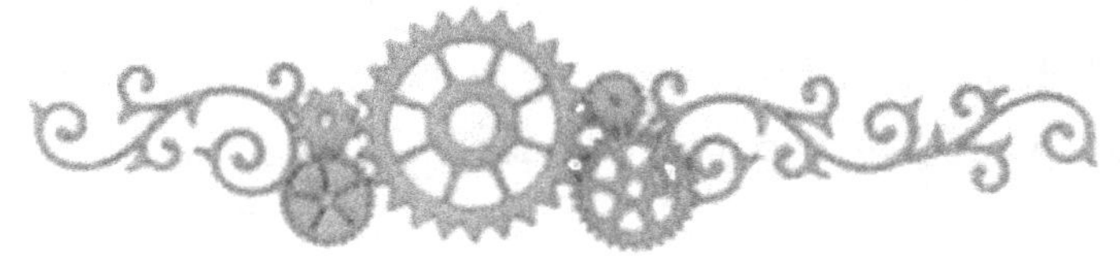

CHAPTER TWENTY-EIGHT

Wherein the spirit of Jebediah Coffin exacts his revenge.

At first, Katie was relieved. Archie seemed to have forgotten all about her in his frantic panic to get the locked door open. But then he must have realized it was futile, that all his frenzied efforts were useless, and he turned toward her, intent on finding someone to blame, someone on whom he might unleash the full wrath of his frustrated anger.

"You caused this! If you'd given in willingly, and accepted me submissively like any decent woman should I wouldn't have had to drag you back to this horrid place. I'm not so bad to look at—you said so once or twice yerself. Maybe not quite as pretty as Mr. Wildethorne, but hell, *I* never deserted you!"

No, you latched onto me like a bloody leach, and you've been sucking the life out of me ever since. I've wanted to be free of you since the day you started hanging around.

"He came after me, didn't he, Archie? Even after I almost got him killed and swore I never wanted to see him again, he came to rescue me. You'd never do that, Archie!"

"Shut up, bitch!" He stalked over to the nearest wall and gave it a good punch. Shaking his bruised fist as he stalked back toward Katie, a nasty taint stained his eyes. "So, I'm stuck in this damned room with you until my boys realize they haven't been paid yet and open this damned door." Undoing and removing his wide leather belt, he flexed it several times, before giving himself a few practice swings, the heavy brass buckle striking an antique walnut cabinet and leaving deep disfiguring gouges. "Guess what we're going to do, Katie my dear, to gobble away the time."

As Archie spoke he moved toward her, his face distorted by the wide grin of a sadist about to indulge. Yet as Katie's eyes grew wide with fear and she prepared to defend herself as best she could, a dark mist began to form behind Archie, gradually coalescing into the leering form of Jebediah Coffin.

Oh dear God! Mother Mary—No!

Archie seemed to realize the intense fear he saw blazing in Katie's eyes wasn't solely because of him. Too late he understood there was something far more menacing hovering just behind him. Whirling around with a snarl, Archie's own piggish eyes opened wide in disbelief as a vengeful Jebediah Coffin charged forward.

Unable to believe what she was somehow hearing, Katie listened as her uncle's ghost declared he'd have his pound of flesh and finally tear the beating, black heart from his murderer.

In spite of the constant clanging and hissing of the chamber's sole radiator and an insistent pounding on the other side of the sealed door, Katie cringed when Archibald Briggs began screaming. Clawing at his chest, he screamed like a madman and began sobbing about being so cold, before suddenly pitching forward and lying deathly still.

While Katie watched in horror, the figure of her murdered uncle rose from the steaming corpse of his killer, threw aside something small and bloody, and drifted across the room toward her, his rapine intent burning in his leering face.

"Ah, revenge is so sweet. But no more silly games, my pretty little niece. Time you gave me what I want!" Jebediah's spirit whined as he stalked toward Katie, his near-corporeal body beginning to lose substance as he advanced.

"Not bloody likely, uncle," Katie vowed, as she caught the phantom lecher between the legs with her raised knee. "You got your revenge on your killer! I'll not be another of your bleeding playthings! "When Jebediah Coffin began to howl in thwarted pain and disintegrate to a sooty mist, Katie kicked him again, adding, "You go straight to hell!"

* * * *

Standing alone in the room, trying to slow her pile-driving heart, Katie stood quivering like a doe transfixed in an oncoming coal truck's headlamps.

She heard the hammering and scraping outside the chamber's door as though some frantic beast was trying to get in, and once or twice she became aware of Scott calling her name. Only when the big radiator off to one side began to clang and percolate like a shrieking teapot did she shake loose her entrancement and realize although the two monsters in her life were dead she was still in terrible danger.

Crying Scott's name, she scooted toward the sealed door.

CHAPTER TWENTY-NINE

Whereas our lovers are about to be torn apart for all time.

The cavalry had arrived. Joshua Steele stormed into Blackbriars manor at the head of a squadron of determined policemen, shipyard workers and mariners. They'd even thought to bring a local midwife, who took immediate charge of Nathaniel, though the whimpering child had to be brought outside to her. The staunch Catholic midwife refused to set one foot inside such an evil place. Instead, they huddled together inside one of the trucks beneath a half dozen moth-eaten blankets. She calmed Nathaniel, singing him old Sicilian lullabies, and clutching her ornate crucifix as she cast a wary eye at the hellish structure before her.

Joshua found Scott easily, following his constant hammering and alarmed cursing of "this damned infernal door". Scott barely looked up from pounding on the door, acknowledging Josh's presence with a nod and watching as their allies spread out through the library and took Archie's henchmen into custody. As soon as Scott knew Nathaniel was being hustled to safety, he resumed his assault on the door, pleading with Katie to answer him.

"Katie! Katie, for the love of Christ, answer me! Are you all right in there?"

Off to one side, Ulysses Truesdale gestured frantically as he shouted at Josh. Scott glanced at them, catching a phrase or two. The Tinman seemed to believe the excessive heat enveloping the manor, and the rising crescendo of clanging agitated pipes and radiators screamed of impending doom. Instead of joining Scott in finding a way to open the jammed door, the two of them moved away, shouting to their comrades that they were all in imminent danger, needing to get out of the manor as fast as possible. The place was a ticking clockwork bomb.

"Scott, listen to me. Stop talking to the damned door a minute, and listen! Do you even know she's still alive in there?"Josh, hesitated a moment, as if the sight of agony in Scott's eyes was too much to bear. When the Tinman moved up behind him, he seemed to find the courage needed to rip Scott's attention from the woman on the other side of the door. "Look, Scott, Tinman figures someone has purposely smashed up all this monstrosity's heating system. Pressure's been building a while, with no place to go! Any time now, the jammed-up furnace and everything is going to explode!"

Scott heard the warning, but saying nothing, turned back to the door and began calling Katie's name.

"Scott, damn you! Come on,--we've got to get out of here!"

"You go! Ulysses, give me that fire ax you brought! Katie—if you can hear me, back away from the door!"

Scott cranked up his arm like a star baseball batter and swung the ax at the door with all his might. At first the ax bit deeply into the richly varnished oak door, showering Scott with severed chunks of wood. But then the ax began to bounce back with a bone-jarring recoil. The damned door had an impenetrable steel layer behind the oak!

"There's no way to get that door open, Scott; you can't bite through steel!" Pleading with his best friend to leave, Josh watched while Ulysses hustled the cops and sailors outside. In moments, only Scott and Josh remained stuck inside the ticking time bomb of a manor. And of course, Miss McBride.

"Scott, I'm sorry, but she's gone. We haven't the equipment or time to cut through that steel. There's no way to get her out—you *know* that! Come on! Save yourself! Your Katie is lost."

"Get yourself out, Josh. Look after my son . . . please. I'm not leaving Katie. I'm never abandoning her again!"

"Scott, this place is going to blow! You've got to . . . ."

"You go, Josh. Now! I won't leave her. Not this time."

Josh shook his head, as if debating trying to force his friend to follow him, finally seeming to realize Scott was entitled to his choice. "You always were a stubborn bastard. Too much romance in your soul

for your own good." He pointed at the steel door before them. "I hope in the end, she realized what a good man she had." Josh swiped at his squinting eyes, as though embarrassed by his salty tears. "Well, I'm proud to have known you, old friend. I'll treat your son as though he were my own."Patting his friend's shoulder, he rose and fled the impending doom.

CHAPTER THIRTY

Before our heroine's very eyes.

Trapped on the other side of the door, Kathleen put her cheek against the hot metal again and strained to hear any new sounds. She'd been listening to Scott and Joshua Steele arguing about the need to leave before a violent explosion. If the shaking and rumbling of the radiator in with her was any indicator, they didn't have long, and she prayed Scott would see the folly of hanging on to his romantic but ridiculous notion of staying with her. He had to save himself. She couldn't let him throw his life away. At least that way she could be certain Nathaniel grew up with a decent, responsible provider for a father. Someone who loved the boy as she always had. God almighty knew she didn't have a hope of escape.

Oh God, Scottie, if only things could've been different.

When she'd first heard Scott pleading with her to search for any hidden latch or button which might release the locking mechanism, she'd scoured the metal door for anything that might set her free. She'd pressed, pulled and twisted all the intricate detail she could find, even going so far as to grasp the disturbing door handle her perverted uncle had installed on her side of the door. A bare-breasted mermaid, of all things. *Figures, the damned sick monster.*

Nothing had happened. She was well and truly trapped. Fucked, as Archie would've quickly sneered.

She heard a sound on the other side of the door. Scott, being foolishly heroic, hadn't left.

"Scottie, you can't still be here? Go! Please! Save yourself!"

"I won't. I can't. I love you, Kathleen."

Katie rocked back on her bum, shocked by the words she'd just heard.

"What did you say, Scott? What did you call me?"

"I said I love you, Kathleen."

Kathleen. I Love You. She thought about snapping it was about time he used her Christian name, and certainly about time he'd mustered up the courage to speak those three magical words and finally tell her how he felt. The old Kathleen certainly would have. But in light of her present circumstances she decided to simply bask in this single ray of comforting sunshine a moment before the grave's icy fingers claimed her . He loved her. He truly loved her. He'd stayed, remaining by her side when all the others had fled, endangering his own life even though it was for a hopeless reason. He was going to die for her.

"Scottie. Scot—I want you to listen to me. You've got to get out of here . . . *now*! I *want* you to go. You've got to leave me now; there's no way I'm getting out of here. Please, if you truly love me, save yourself and raise our son. Will you please do that for me? Please."

After a long hesitation that Katie was sure included tears, Scott answered her in a voice that broke her heart. "Y-yes, I'll go. I'll love and raise our son, see that he becomes a fine young man you'd be proud of. N-neither of us will ever forget his mother. I love you with all my heart, Kathleen McBride."

"I love you too," she sobbed. "Now, GO!"

She heard him struggle to his feet, his own voice choked with tears and shards from his shattered heart. But he didn't falter. He was going. *Thank God. I pray it's not too late!*

Katie waited for a few heartbeats, her cheek and palm pressed against the hot metal door as she listened to her lover forcing himself to safety. Oh how she wanted to ooze through the steel and chase after him. At least she knew the two men in her life were safe.

Resigned to the inevitable, she shoved herself away from the barrier, intending to retreat to one of the chairs furthest from the heartless corpse of Archibald Briggs and await her fate.

Only as she rose did she become aware of the young woman rising right by her side, her worried face inches away, staring at her. Dressed in the attire of a serving maid from some bygone era, Katie realized she could see through her. *Why now? Why now should I see spirits the way Scott does? Is it because I'm about to join her? What does she want?*

As if reading her thoughts, the maid moved closer, extending one hand to point at the lascivious doorknob. When Katie's face showed no glimmer of comprehension and she made no move to touch the knob, the spirit exhaled in icy exasperation against a mirror hung between two disgusting paintings. Katie turned, watching the specter scrawl something across the mirror's murky surface. With the mirror frosted over, she hastily scrawled the single word, *Run.*

"That's easy for you to say. You're not trapped in here like a rat. I suppose you could just drift through the door. I'm afraid for me, that's quite impossible—"

Exasperation spreading across her translucent face, the maid shook her finger repeatedly at the doorknob.

Having no idea what the specter wanted, Katie watched in befuddlement as the frustrated maid's spirit glided across the room and positioned herself in front of the door. As Katie watched, the ghost turned to the doorknob, pressed the mermaid's right breast twice and then twisted her tail to the left. The sealed door clicked open immediately. Turning to thank her vanishing savior, Katie swiped the stinging tears from her eyes and fled through the open doorway toward freedom.

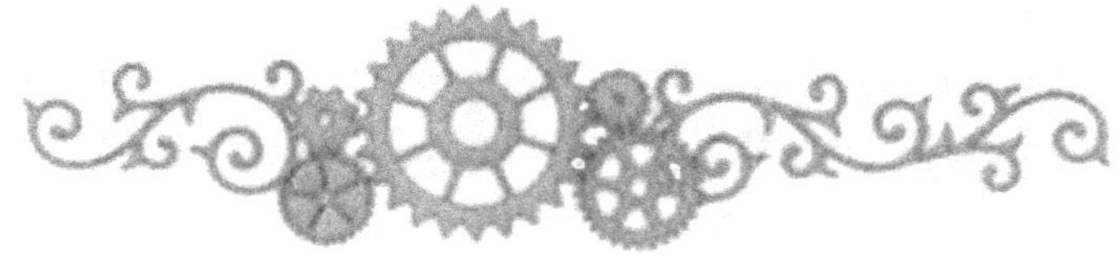

CHAPTER THIRTY-ONE

Wherein everything goes Boom!

Scott was heading back to make one more valiant attempt to free Katie when the house exploded. He'd just handed Nathan back to the Sicilian woman, shrugged off Josh's restraining grasp and started up the path to the ominous mansion when he thought he saw a slight figure scurrying out of the house's gloom. In the next second Blackbriars blew up, the entire manor house disintegrating in a fireball that blew Scott and half the waiting cluster of friends behind him off their feet.

Scott's first concern was for his son, who miraculously remained asleep, cuddled in the protective cocoon provided by the midwife's massive forearms. Checking on Josh, Ulysses and the other men now pulling themselves to their feet, Scott determined no one had sustained more than superficial cuts and bruises. As the fires died down and the stormy wind chased most of the smoke away, he realized all hadn't been so lucky. What little remained standing of Blackbriars was a smoking ruin. Of the figure he'd thought he saw fleeing the manor just before the explosion, there wasn't a sign.

Scott lingered a moment, hoping against all reason, then started to turn away to reclaim his son, his mind seized-up with shock.

Nathaniel was all that remained of the woman he loved, a love he'd finally given voice to moments before he lost her. As he turned, a distant figure popped up, barely visible at the rim of his blurred vision. It squeaked out a name, and promptly fell back down. But Scott's attention stirred, as a zombie senses fresh meat. The figure staggered to its feet again, called his name, and added, "If it's not too much trouble, a lady could use some help here," before falling on her burnt bustle again.

Scott found her in a dozen strides, cradled her in his arms, and smothered her face in kisses as he murmured, "Katie, Katie, thank God you're alive."

"Actually, I think it's a ghost you'll have to thank." Katie winced as Scott lifted her in his arms and started to rise. "Easy there, sailor. I think I've broken my ankle."

"Oh Katie, I thought sure I'd lost you."

"I see you've managed to lose my proper name again. *Kathleen* too much of a challenge I guess. You said it so sweetly too. I suppose those other three words you whispered to me when it looked like I'd be dying would stick in your craw now too?"

"Actually, Katie, I was thinking of adding a few more."

"Oh? And what would those be, my handsome boyo?"

"Kathleen McBride, will you do me the honor of marrying me?"

Suddenly speechless, Katie let herself sink into his strong arms, gradually managing to whisper, "Of course, you thick-headed Yankee. I thought you'd never get around to asking."

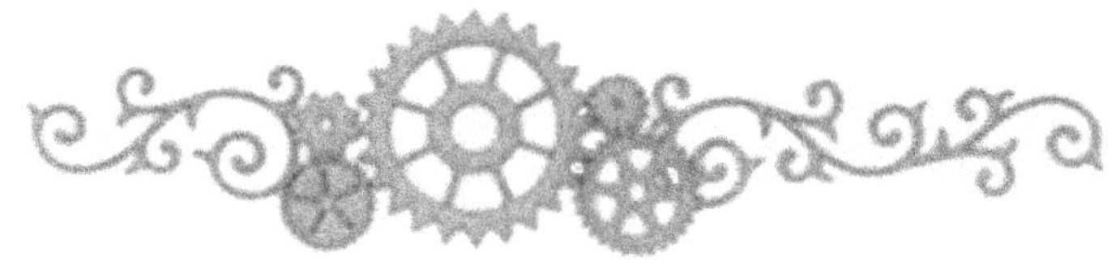

THE END...ALMOST

Scott and Katie married within a fortnight, surrounded by a sea of friends. It can't be said that they'd live happily ever after; that being the stuff of children's' fairytales, but they did very well together, adding a daughter and another son to their crew, and managing to keep their love and passion for each other alive and well for all their years. As for Blackbriars, that blight on Newport's coastline was eventually leveled and turned into Wildethorne's aeronautical and marine shipyards. Although most of the contracts for airships came from the Navy and Coast Guard, Scott did produce a number of lucrative airships for Newport's idle rich. Over time rumors grew of phantoms seen wandering the airfield grounds on foggy nights, and the occasional ghostly figure drifting along the empty passageways inside one or two of the larger dirigibles. Since the corpse of Horace Gaunt had never been found, some local busybodies spread the rumor it might be him, a fledgling serial murderer in his own right, seeking fresh victims. But those are tales for another time, still lurking impatiently in the mist-shrouded aether.

The End. Really this time.

Creator of *Siren's Song*, his first adventure novel, and now *Like Clockwork*, a Gothic steampunk romance, Wayne grew up and lives in the New England area he writes about. Being a scuba diver, award-winning creator and painter of military, fantasy and steampunk miniatures as well as love of his family and husky keep him pretty busy, yet he still makes time to write. He still harbors his childhood notion that love should win, and there are things hiding in the back of his closet. Once in a while, he lets them out.